W9-BPJ-830

Publisher's Note

F   30301
Hol
        Holland, Robert.

        Footballs never bounce
        true.

DATE DUE

NOV 16			
SEP 8 '09			
SEP 22 '09			
OCT 6 '10			

DISCARD
H.S
No. Judson, IN 46366

DEMCO

as
on
at
lik
bo

pl
st
m

pr
Th
an
lei
qu

m
up
qu

y
co
lo

on
h

b
ch
al

, though
use the
s aimed
rls also
e of any

ig, sim-
end the
ven ro-
ence.

-appro-
ate kid.
ructure
le chal-
aise the

it, fair-
e, screw
hich re-

els for
be dis-
ch yel-

printed
e rough

only a
might
rs, after
er.

First Edition

All rights reserved. No part of this book may be reproduced by any means, except as allowed by copyright statutes or in writing by the publisher. This is a work of fiction and any resemblance to anyone, living or dead, is purely coincidental.

Book Illustration and design by Robert J. Benson
Woodland Creative Group
Montgomery Center, Vermont

Text set in Palatino

Copyright 1999 by Robert Holland
Printed in Quebec, Canada

ISBN 0 - 965852342

Footballs Never Bounce True

F Hol
Footballs never bounce true :

30301
NJ-SP High School Media Center

A novel of Sports and Mystery by
Robert Holland

FROST HOLLOW PUBLISHERS, LLC
Woodstock, Connecticut

No. Judson-San Pierre H.S
900 Campbell Drive
No. Judson, IN 46366

30301

More
"Books boys want to read"
by Robert Holland

The Voice of the Tree
Summer on Kidd's Creek
The Purple Car

Chapter One

Larry the Rat

If Damon Foxrucker had kept his mouth shut, he would never have met Larry the Rat, but he could no more have done that than he could have sprouted wings.

He was just one of those guys who talked himself into trouble. To begin with, he didn't like rules. Well, does anyone like rules? Has there ever been a kid who liked rules? The only reason they follow them is because if they don't, adults get on their case, and they wind up being grounded or forced to do some unpleasant task like emptying the garbage. Damon particularly hated emptying the garbage. He hated it so much he'd offered to surrender his allowance if his folks would put in a garbage disposal, but his mom was on a big environmental kick, and all he got was a long lecture on being responsible for the environment, and how it was better to throw the garbage in the dump than put it in the septic tank. That didn't make any sense to Damon, because his science teachers claimed that dumps rated right up there with devil worship. But what did he know? He was just a kid, right? Fourteen going on fifteen. Nowhere. Too young by forever to drive, too young to do this, too young to do that, and far too old to act like a kid.

He'd tried the anti-dump argument on his father, but it was like trying to move a brick with a feather. He didn't agree or disagree, he just ignored it. His mother said he was not thinking logically, but that was what she said about any thought he had.

Which was part of why Damon had decided that life sucked. There was also the matter of his name. Bad name. In eighth grade not a day had gone by that someone didn't get on his case about his name, and usually that had led to trouble of some kind, which was partly why his folks had decided to send him to high school in Wally's Falls. At least that's what his mother kept telling him, but when she explained it to anyone else, she said it was that the high school in Fayette wasn't competitive enough, and she wanted to be sure that Damon got into a good college. She was very big on good colleges, having gone East to Vassar. His father had been the greatest running back ever at Wally's Falls, and then he had gone into the Marines and fought in a war. Damon understood, without anyone admitting to the truth, that the real reason he was going to Wally's Falls was to play football. In Fayette they played soccer.

That they could choose between the school systems in either town was the result of where they lived. The town line went through the exact middle of the house. He did not mention football, nor did he mention the fact that aside from math, his grades, like his life, seemed sort of low grade. His mother did not like football. She was confused. Not that she was unusual in that regard, because all adults were confused, but she seemed more dense than usual on the subject of football. But now that he thought about it, she hadn't even gotten it clear yet that he was a boy, he was big, and he was an athlete.

As evidence of adult confusion, he often pointed to a study that showed how teenagers liked to stay up late and get up late. It wasn't their fault, according to the study, but had to do with their biological clock. The gist of the article was that kids would do better in school if they started later and stayed later in the day. The mistake had been in raising the issue in science class after the school board had decided to start school an hour earlier. Mr. Mashee sent him to the office.

And then he got into it again in the next class when he asked Ms Quint, his social studies teacher, why the board had done something so dumb.

"There's nothing dumb about it," she said. "It's better for the school, it's better for parents, and it's better for teachers."

"But it isn't good for kids," he said.

The idea so took her by surprise, that all she could do was huff and puff like a fat old toad. "Well (huff) I can't (puff), I mean (huff) see why (puff)...."

"I think we should take a vote," he said.

"This is not a democracy!" she shouted back.

"But the guy who wrote the article is a doctor," Damon said. "He must know what's right."

"It just isn't logical," she said.

"Why not?"

"You're missing the point."

Adults, Damon thought, are big on kids missing the point, and yet they seldom do. He decided to humor her. "What is the point?" he asked.

"The point is that this is my job. It's my livelihood!"

"Which is more important," he asked, "how something affects your job, or how something affects how kids learn?"

His classmates cheered, and that did in Ms Quint, who insisted on being called Ms instead of Mrs., a point which Damon had contested in the first week of school, because it also meant having to write "he/she" in his essays.

Damon," she had said, "that is a perfectly logical construction, and you will use it!"

"It isn't in the dictionary," he had said.

"That is of no consequence."

"I'd like a second opinion," he'd said, and that's when she had sent him off to see the principal.

And now it was close to happening again. "Damon, you have to learn some respect for authority."

"Even when it doesn't make any sense?"

"I'm sending you to the principal," she said.

Mr. Waters looked up from his desk as Damon entered his office. "Ah, Foxrucker," he said. "A perfect record today. Two classes and two trips to my office."

The word on Mr. Waters was that he was a good guy. He'd played baseball all the way to triple-A, and he fished and hunted, and not a father in town didn't think he was the best principal they'd ever had. Which meant the mothers hated him. Well, not all of them, because some of them had sons in the Marines, and they understood about how boys respect the big dog.

And Harmon Waters was a big dog. He stood nearly six-five and when he squared his broad shoulders and scowled, you felt like you wanted to find a hole real fast. Men who act like men are surprisingly unpopular with married women.

But not even one of the guys he'd thrown out of school, and there were plenty of those because Wally's Falls was an old mill town with more than its share of tough guys, had anything bad to say about Mr. Waters. When he laid things out, it was all understandable. If he caught you breaking the rules, you paid the price. No excuses.

That he hadn't gotten thrown out, Damon regarded as a miracle, but in fact Harmon Waters had never considered it, despite some pointed remarks from the head of the teacher's union about student disrespect. Mr. Waters regarded Damon as a special case. Granted he had a big mouth, but his thinking always seemed so clear and fair that all he could do was listen carefully, smile, and send Damon back to class. There was also the matter of football, because this was, after all, Harley Foxrucker's boy, and that meant football. More importantly, it meant winning, and it had been a long dry spell at good old Wally's Falls, a dry spell that he expected to see end with Damon. The word was out. He could throw the football, and all he needed was the chance. That raised another issue, but he had decided to deal with that when it came up.

"You are a strange guy, Damon," Mr. Waters said. "Most guys that get sent down here have done something I can do something about, but it's very hard for me to tell you not to get into these arguments with your teachers." He turned around and hit several keys on his computer. "But what I don't understand is how your arguments can be so solid and your grades, with the exception of algebra, so mediocre. Can you explain that?"

Damon shrugged. The shrug is very important, and he was an expert at shrugging. His mother's mother, who was pretty stiff for a grandmother, opposed shrugging and every time he shrugged, she'd say, "stop shrugging, young man." And usually he just shrugged again, and then she'd turn to his mother. "Grace, tell Damon not to shrug. It is very impolite." And then his mom would say, "Damon, don't shrug." And then he'd shrug.

"You can do better than that," Mr. Waters said.

"I don't check my work," he said.

"And what else?"

"Sometimes I don't do it."

"Why?"

"Have you read any of these books, sir?"

Mr. Waters' eyes grew wider in anticipation.

"I gotta tell you, sir, they are very boring."

Mr. Waters nodded. "I agree with you. Very boring. Dull enough to put a librarian to sleep. But that doesn't matter, does it?"

"It should."

"But it doesn't."

"Just cause I'm a kid."

"Yup. Absolutely right. Our job is to make sure you don't stay a kid, and the way we do that is to bore you to death, so that you want to get on with things and get to be an adult. Then you can spend your time boring kids."

Damon grinned. You couldn't help but grin when Mr. Waters talked that way. He didn't lie, and he made things understandable, even when they didn't make any sense.

"Damon, you just have to put up with this and trust us not to feed you stuff because we delight in seeing kids suffer. I won't deny that some of our teachers like to make their students squirm, but for most of us, the only thing we have in mind is making sure you get the best education we can offer ... and ..."

He was interrupted by a dull, thudding sound, and he ran to the window to watch a great cloud of oily black smoke come pouring from the chemistry lab windows. Seconds later the fire alarm went off.

"Damn! It must be Thursday." Mr. Waters dashed around his desk and out the door.

Damon followed, hoping he wouldn't be noticed. As they ran to the stairs and down to the ground floor, they passed teachers and students filing out of the building. The smoke hung in a black haze in the hallway, and they had to duck under it, and Damon was beginning to think maybe he'd be better off outside, when Mr. Potter burst out of the chem lab, waving his arms as he swam through the smoke.

"It's okay!" he shouted. "It's okay! There's no fire!" But with his eyes stuck on extra-wide-open, he did not look as if everything were okay.

In the distance they could hear the siren sound at the volunteer fire station at the bottom of the hill.

Suddenly Mr. Potter threw his arms up over his head and screamed. "We need to ventilate! We need to ventilate!" He sounded like a cat with its tail closed in the door.

"Sounds like you already are," Mr. Waters said.

Mr. Potter was beyond the reach of humor.

"Perkins again?" Mr. Waters asked.

"It's Thursday isn't it?" Mr. Potter screeched. "That kid is a disaster! Every Thursday he blows up something else. You've got to get him out of chemistry!"

Damon thought those were pretty sweet words. To get out of chemistry, all you had to do was blow up the lab. He had never thought life could be so simple.

It wasn't. "You know we can't do that, Tom," Mr. Waters said. "Every kid in the place will try to blow up the lab in order to get kicked out of chemistry."

Mr. Potter was beginning to calm as the smoke began to wane. "There has to be a way, Harmon, there just has to! This simply can't go on."

Just then Larry Perkins appeared, sailing ghost-like from the smoke, holding a beaker pouring more black smoke into the air. "I'VE GOT IT!" he shouted, and then raised his right hand, closed it into a fist, and jerked it downward. "YES!"

His face was covered with black soot, except where his safety glasses had left two white rings. That made him odd enough looking to make anyone laugh, but in fact, Larry Perkins was an odd looking guy, however you measured him. He had a big nose that seemed to pull his face outward with it and his ears stuck out and he looked like a ... rat. Damon liked him right from the start. He was wild and contagious.

Damon fanned away the smoke and looked more closely at this improbable, short, skinny guy, who had the strangest eyes he had ever seen. They were violet, and the irises were streaked with silver that flashed and danced in the light.

Perkins had caught the two men so off guard that they couldn't react before he wheeled and disappeared back into the smoke.

"Perkins!" Mr. Potter roared.

"Yes, sir. Just be a second. I have to stabilize this stuff!"

"Does he know what he's doing?" Mr. Waters asked.

"He knows more chemistry that I do, it's just that he keeps blowing things up! And he refuses to do any of the regular experiments, and..."

Mr. Waters looked around at Damon. "Sounds like your kind of guy," he said.

Damon shrugged.

"He's new this year, same as you are."

From the way Mr. Waters looked at him, Damon knew something unpleasant was about to complicate his life.

"A couple of new guys, maybe you could talk to him."

"Why me?" He might have liked Larry Perkins, but clearly the guy was a geek, and you had to be careful about getting chummy with geeks.

"Maybe you could make him understand about how we frown on people blowing up the chemistry lab."

"He looks like a rat," Damon said. Maybe if he was the starting quarterback it'd be okay to hang out with a rat, but after four weeks he was on the bench, and he wasn't even listed as a quarterback. Coach hadn't let him even try out at quarterback because he already had two. What that came down to was simply that his reputation was vulnerable.

It must have shown in his expression.

"Tell you what," Mr. Waters said. "I've got a deal for you. You talk to Larry about not sabotaging the chem lab, and I'll tell Mrs. Quint that you don't have to use 'he/she' in your essays."

Damon grinned. "Deal," he said, still uncertain whether he had won or lost, but guessing that just being able to make such a deal with the principal was going to work in his favor. Sooner or later someone was going to make some crack about his name and there was gonna be trouble. Not a fight, but something. Fighting got you kicked off everything.

Lost in his thoughts, he walked back to class along with the other kids, talking and chattering as they came in from the fire drill. He wondered how long it would take to know even half of them. The hardest part was going to be finding a date for the prom in November. No, the hardest part would be finding someone to double with, because there was no way he was going to have his mother driving him to the prom. Out of the question. And even if he found someone to double with, he still had to get a date, and most likely she had to be a freshman, because upper class girls did not date freshmen.

As he rounded the corner he almost collided with a girl he hadn't seen before. Only his quickness allowed him to avoid a full head-on collision, dodging just enough to keep from knocking her down, though he still sideswiped her arm, turning her toward him, and causing her to drop her backpack.

"Whoa, sorry," he said, and then all he could do was stare like some kind of simpleton. She was so pretty she took his breath away. Her hair was long and black and very shiny, and her light hazel eyes seemed to glow with an inner light. And she was angry.

"Why don't you watch where you're going!" She bent to retrieve her backpack.

"I ... I'm sorry," he said.

She snatched up the backpack. "Well you can't just go around knocking people ..." she looked at him for the first time.

He smiled. "I really am sorry."

She softened quickly and a smile began to appear. "Are all football players like you?"

"Maybe I should start at the beginning here. Hi, I'm Damon Foxrucker."

"I know who you are."

"You do?"

She smiled. "I'm Jenny Simmons. Our little sisters are good friends."

"They are? Wow! I never knew that."

"I'm also trying out for cheerleading, and it helps to know

who you are going to be cheering for."

"Won't be me," Damon said. "I'll be lucky to get off the bench once the whole season."

"But your sister says you're a great player."

"She said that? Belle said that?"

"She did."

"I didn't think she knew anything about football."

Jenny grinned in the way girls have of grinning that makes you think they know something when they don't. Usually, it pissed him off but now he only grinned back. "I'm sorry about running into you."

"It's okay."

And then his brain went into scramble mode and he couldn't think of anything to say. How come he couldn't just come up with a line like the guys did in the movies, something smart and smooth?

Jenny took over. "It's just a good thing we didn't hit head on. They'd have had to helicopter me to the hospital."

He laughed and he could not have stopped smiling if he had wanted to.

The crowd in the hall had thinned to a trickle as the students returned to their classes.

"I gotta get to class," Jenny said.

"Are you okay?"

"I'm fine," she said. "But I really do have to get to class."

"Yeah, me too." He looked down at his feet. "I'll see you, okay?"

"Okay." She turned away and walked off down the hall, and as he watched her walk away, there wasn't the least doubt in his mind about who he was gonna ask to the prom.

Chapter Two

Footballs Never Bounce True

If ever, Damon thought, a place sounded like wussville it was Wally's Falls, which meant that when you played football for the Wally's Falls Beavers, you had to be tough, if only because the name of the school was so bad. No wonder the football team didn't win anymore. Maybe a name like Wally's Falls was okay when his dad was on the team, because old people from those times never noticed stuff like that. But this was modern times, and kids noticed everything now. And as if the name of the town wasn't bad enough they had a beaver for a mascot, not a real beaver, but a guy dressed up in a beaver suit. To win games, you had to have a mascot that was nasty and mean. Beavers did not exactly have a reputation as fierce or nasty. And around here, he thought, everyone knows that beavers are so dumb that a lot of the time they get whacked by the tree they're chewing down. No. You had to have a mascot like a grizzly or a wolf or maybe a cougar.

Damon finished his laps and trotted in toward the bench, noticing as he jogged along, that somebody was lying on the ground near the bench while the trainer worked on his leg. But that was nothing new. Somebody was always throwing a charley horse and, hey, when you play football, you get hurt.

"Okay," Coach Bunker said, as he stood with his hands on his hips. He was short and round, and his huge stomach bulged out over his shorts like an avalanche waiting to happen. The baseball cap on his balding head pushed his gray hair out above his ears like miniature wings, and when he talked he shouted like the old men who had spent their lives in the brass stamping mill when they didn't wear ear protectors. "We'll start with the usual drills. Until we find out how bad Montville got hurt tripping over the bench, Foxrucker will be the backup quarterback."

Nobody laughed. Not that there wasn't something funny about a football player getting injured by tripping over the bench, because there was, and for sure Montville was gonna hear about it. But the real reason nobody laughed was because Coach Bunker's usual way of dealing with anyone who disagreed with him was to bite chunks out of them.

But there was yet another reason nobody laughed. Curiosity. The new kid was going to play at quarterback; the kid with the big mouth, the nasty name, and the reputation for being able to throw a football. But while everybody had heard that he could throw, nobody had ever seen him throw a football, so they assumed he couldn't, and they were all enjoying the prospect of seeing him screw up so Coach Bunker could holler at him. And what made that funny was that after Coach Bunker had been dragged in front of the school board for using "inappropriate language," he had assigned Mr. Zander, his assistant coach, to stand next to him when he was chewing someone out and blast an air horn every time he swore, so nobody could hear what he said. Sometimes the blasts lasted fifteen or twenty seconds, and the effect, because of the way Coach Bunker's face went red as an August tomato, was to make you think that he was the power that drove the air horn, instead of the aerosol can attached to the bottom of it. In truth, the air horn had no effect, because Coach Bunker only shouted louder each time he swore, and he had a voice the equal of any foghorn.

Damon didn't know anything about Coach Bunker's temper or his picturesque language, but their first game was a week away, and Damon wondered, as he walked toward the bench, if would even get a chance to play. Most likely he'd end up sitting on the bench, or maybe run a few plays at tailback. Like Dad had said, when you're the new guy, it sometimes doesn't matter how good you are, because coaches start the kids they know.

Usually, he didn't pay too much attention when Dad went off on one of his talks, but this time it looked like he'd told him the truth, though, to be honest, he couldn't think of a time when he hadn't. But at least he'd made the varsity, and he was the only freshman on the team. Probably his size had helped, not to mention the fact that because he'd been born in December, his parents had started him a year later, so he was older than the other kids in his class.

He watched the starting offense and defense take the field, and then walked over and picked up a ball. After four weeks of practice he'd gotten to know the guys on the team pretty well, and he had earned some respect for his ability to carry the ball, even if he wasn't a jack rabbit. He could also take a hit and he could dish it out too.

He looked at the guys sitting on the bench and picked one out. "Hey, Warren, I need to warm up."

Warren Wilson looked up, smiled and shook his head. "Throw what? You don't mean a football, do you? Hey, Foxrucker, haven't you got it yet? Nobody throws footballs on this team."

"Well, I thought I might like to change that," Damon said.

Only because he was curious, did Warren get up and stand ready to catch the ball. But Damon never got it off.

"Foxrucker," Bunker shouted. "What the BLAAAT do you

think you're doing! I want you to sit there and watch and go over the BLAAAT-ing play book."

Damon, startled by the air horn, looked back at Warren. "What the heck was that?"

Warren grinned. "The school board outlawed swearing."

"You're serious, right?"

"Serious, man. Wait'll we get into the season and we start losing games. The air horn goes all the time."

Damon looked at the ball bag thirty feet away, cocked his arm, and tossed the ball in a perfect spiral into the open maw of the bag. It popped back out and rolled off in typical willy-nilly football fashion. He shrugged, walked to the end of the bench, picked up the play book, sat down, and opened it to the first page. He knew it cold. He might not have his French vocab down, but he knew this book from front to back. What he didn't know was the guys he was playing with, especially the offensive linemen and the receivers. Only once had Coach gone over pass plays in practice, and the only plays he called were the desperation plays you used near the end of the game after nothing else had worked. Even those bombs weren't very long because Ricky Hayes threw like a girl.

He looked out at the field. Not even the running plays were working now, even against their own defense, which had more holes in it than the colander his mother used to drain the spaghetti. Which meant that sooner or later he'd get in, and when he did he was gonna throw. But to do that he was gonna have to ignore the play Coach sent in, and there was no better way to wind up on the bench for the rest of the year. But maybe, just maybe, once Coach saw him throw, it'd be different.

He flipped the pages to the section of the book for pass patterns. Four. All simple. Throw the ball and let the receiver run under it. The worst part was that he knew how to play this game, even if he hadn't ever played anything but touch. His dad and both his uncles had played, and they had taught him how to throw and how to block and how to run. Every summer when they spent a month at the shore with the whole family, and all they did was swim, fish, play football, and shoot skeet. But he was the new guy, the freshman, and his job was to follow orders, and if there was one thing in this world that gave him trouble, it was following orders. His fourth grade teacher had even tried to get him classified as a special ed student because he wouldn't follow orders.

Everybody compared him to his sister Carrie, who had gotten wonderful grades and followed all the rules, and gone on to a good college in the East. But now he was the oldest, and he was supposed to set an example for Belle, who was four years younger. But what kind of an example could he set for his cute little sister, who got very high grades, and followed all the rules, and most of the time was pretty nice to him? On the other hand she knew Jenny Simmons and if girls did nothing else, they talked. He shook his head. Too complicated. How could anyone deal with anything that complicated?

Stick with football. In football you followed the coach's rules and you kept your mouth shut, or you never got the chance to play. Mouthing off in class was nothing compared to this, because he really didn't care whether he got thrown out of class, but he did not want to get thrown off the football team. That was the future. Grades only mattered because his mom was a tiger about keeping his grades up, even though grades didn't really count when you could throw a football like he could. And he was already six feet tall and a hundred and eighty pounds, and he figured that ought to mean six-four and two-ten by the time he was a senior. Guys like that got big-time scholarships. He looked up from the play book. "Hey, Warren, you're a wide receiver, right?"

Warren grinned, his teeth startlingly white against his dark skin. "All I do is run back punts." He laughed. "Last year I only got to run back two, because we were so bad that the other teams never had to punt. I should be out there now, but Coach plays two big tight ends to improve the blocking."

Damon shook his head. "Not good," he said.

"We've got some good players," Warren said, "and we've even got a pretty good offensive line, but all we do is run for three plays and punt, run for three plays and punt."

"Ricky hasn't got much of an arm, Damon said.

"Weak ... very weak."

"Is that why Coach only calls running plays?"

"Naw. Last year we had a guy who could throw pretty good, but Coach never called a single pass play the whole season. And you know what? We scored four touchdowns, the whole season. It was a state record."

"Quarterbacks throw passes," Damon said.

"All right, take a BLAAAT-ing break!"

Damon waited for him to reach the sidelines, then walked over. "Coach?"

"Yeah?"

"I wondered, when I go in, could I try a couple of passes?"

"Passes! Only BLAAAT-heads play the game that way! Football is called football because you use your BLAAAT-ing feet!"

"Yes, sir."

"And make sure you remember that!"

"Yes, sir."

Not that it mattered, because he never got onto the field. Everybody else on the team got at least a few minutes, but he got nothing. What he did get, however, was some time to think and watch, and he guessed that Ricky Hayes was not gonna last long without getting hurt. It wasn't that he played badly. He just looked as if he didn't like contact, and guys like that always got hurt because they weren't ready to get hit. And Montville's knee didn't look good at all. Too much swelling. Which meant that sooner or later he'd get to play, and he decided he was gonna be ready. The plan began to uncoil in his mind like a snake slowly revealing its length. Yeah, he'd be ready and so would Warren and the rest of the guys. But it would be tricky, because it meant he'd have to call a private practice so his dad could teach them how to pass block and how to run patterns. If he'd do it. No. He'd never got over playing football, even if he hadn't played beyond high school. When you looked at the record books for Wally's Falls, Dad held all the rushing records. When Harley Foxrucker got the football it had taken three and four guys to bring him down. And his brother, Phil, had been the quarterback, and they had gone undefeated four years in a row. In those days when other teams had to play the Wally's Falls Beavers nobody laughed. They just got sick to their stomachs, knowing what a nasty day they had ahead of them. But that was twenty-six years ago, and they'd had a different coach then.

When high school ended Harley went into the Marines. Had he even considered going to college? Or was it just not what Foxruckers did? They fixed engines and sold cars and trucks and motorcycles, and they made more money than most guys who went to college. But it raised a question, and one day he'd need an answer. Not yet, because just now he didn't want to cloud the issue. It was gonna take his best argument because it wasn't gonna take Dad long to figure out that they were going against their coach, and he was very, very big on following the coach's orders. Mouthing off was one thing, but in Dad's book, you never mouthed off at a coach. The boss called the shots.

But Damon wasn't only a Foxrucker, he was a Whitman too, and that side of the family did a lot of negotiating.

Of course there was one other small problem and that was getting the other guys on the team to turn up. Bottom line ... he was still a freshman, and upperclassmen didn't listen to freshmen. Somehow he had to convince Warren and Roger, Joe and

Melvin that this would work, and the best place to get to them was in the locker room after paractice.

After they'd showered and were getting dressed, he homed in on Warren and Roger who had lockers next to each other. He stood, leaning against the lockers with one hand. "Hey, you guys," he said, "it's really true about Bunker isn't it, I mean the part about not allowing any passes."

"It's true," Warren said, flashing his broad grin, his teeth flashing white against his mahogany skin. "The rumor is you got a real strong arm."

Damon shrugged.

"And an ugly name," Roger said, testing Damon to see whether he'd rise.

But Damon only grinned. "Nobody Foxruckers with my name. And spoonerisms are very dangerous."

"Spoonerism? What's a spoonerism?" Warren grinned. "Sounds like something you eat with."

"Be better if it were," Damon said.

"What are you thinking?" Roger asked. "That you're gonna throw a pass if you get in?" He combed his blond hair.

"Yeah."

"What makes you think he'll put you in?" Warren said. "You're still only a freshman, you know."

"Montville's out for the season, and ...."

"How do you know that?"

"I'm pretty sure he tore some cartilage."

"That still leaves Ricky," Roger said.

Damon shrugged. "Ricky won't last. He runs away from contact and that's gonna get him hurt."

"He made it through last year," Warren said.

"But he didn't play much," Roger said. He looked at Damon. "And you're right, he'll get blindsided."

"And that's why we keep fumbling the handoffs," Warren said. "He's stepping away." He stood up. "You didn't come over here to tell us that. What's on your mind, here?"

"I thought, if you guys wanted, I could get my dad to draw up a few pass plays for us, and maybe we could practice them on Sunday in the park. That way, if I got into a game and we got the chance maybe we could pull something off. But if we don't practice them, it'll never work 'cause we won't know the timing. I mean, I need to know how fast you guys run and how quick you make your cuts, stuff like that."

"You're crazy, Foxrucker," Roger said.

"No, Rog, now wait a minute here. I think he makes sense. And this might be our only chance in high school to catch a pass. Maybe we ought to think about it."

Roger laughed and shook his head. "Go against Bunker? Warren, I think you're losing it, you know that?"

"Well what else is there? We're both wide receivers who never get to play wide receiver, right? What's the fun in that?"

"I don't know."

"We'd need Joe Santos to center the ball, and Melvin Upshaw at tight end," Damon said.

"And you want us to talk them into doing this?" Roger said.

Damon shook his head. "Yeah, I know crazy, right? I know I'm out of line here, being a freshman and all, but I thought it was worth a shot."

"Wait a minute," Roger said. "Your dad must be Harley Foxrucker, is that right?"

"Yup."

"Maybe that puts a different light on things."

"Who's Harley Foxrucker?" Warren asked.

"Stop by the trophy case in the hall, Warren. The guy holds every rushing record for the school and they went undefeated for four years when he was here." He looked around at Damon. "I wondered where you learned to fake like that."

"That's all I can do. I can scramble, but I'm way too slow to be a running back. You guys, on the other hand, can fly."

"And your dad will work with us?" Roger asked.

"Yeah."

Roger looked around at Warren. "This could be fun, you know that?"

"Hey, don't talk to me," Warren said, "I'm already signed on. All I do is run back punts, and all I want to do is catch passes. What have I got to lose?"

"Sunday you said."

"One o'clock in the park. In the outfield."

Roger shook his head. "Is this crazy? I think this is crazy, but I'm in. Warren and I will talk to Joe and Melvin. No matter what happens they can't get benched. He still needs a center and Joe is too good. Besides, who could tell if he was part of it? Even Melvin can't get hurt here. Most of the time he's just another blocker."

Damon grinned. "All right."

"You're sure you can throw," Warren asked.

"Here," Damon said, "I'll show you." He opened his bag and pulled out a ball. "You go stand by the shower room and I'll go up to the front."

"Okay," Warren said, that's what, maybe a hundred feet?"

Roger nodded. "And the ceiling is only eight feet and the space is maybe three feet wide. That's a tough throw, Foxrucker. Some guys couldn't do that with a baseball, let alone a football."

"I've been throwing footballs since I was five," Damon said. He walked to the front of the locker room, holding the ball in his big hand, the fingers reaching over half way round the ball. When he turned Warren was standing at the far end and Damon simply cocked his arm and threw a perfect spiral the length of the room. It was very flat, which meant it was also going very fast, but that didn't bother Warren. He just watched it into his hands.

Roger hooted and then laughed. "All right! It's on!"

I'll talk to you tomorrow," Damon said.

"Yeah," Roger said. "Tomorrow."

Chapter Three

Blowing Up the Bus

They sat in the back of the late East bus, Damon and three soccer players, their hair still wet from the shower, talking about this and that. They were all freshmen, which accounted for having the back seats to themselves. The older kids did not ride the bus. They either drove or they had friends who drove.

And because he hadn't gone to school with the soccer players, and because they were talking about soccer, Damon sat and looked down the long aisle toward the front of the bus. The afternoon had clouded over, and he thought it would probably rain during the night. The falling barometer pretty well matched his mood. He didn't even care at the moment whether practice got rained out or not. What was the point? If he couldn't throw the ball, he couldn't see any point in staying on the team. Maybe he'd have to go away to school. What a bummer. If he went away, he'd have to give up driving his monster machine, and he wouldn't be able to hunt in the fall. Bummer. His only hope now rested with Warren and Roger. If they'd just try one practice, if they once saw how he could throw, he was sure they'd take the risk. But first they had to come to the park on Sunday. Okay. He needed a strategy.

"Hey, Damon," Dan Fearing said, "how's life with Bunker?"

"Three plays and punt ... three plays and punt."

"No ball carriers?"

"Oh, we got ball carriers," Damon said, "but we wear 'em under out pants."

It absolutely cracked them up. And it got even funnier when Will Jenkins didn't get it.

"I don't get it," Will said.

"Jocks! You idiot!" Charlie Taylor said

Will grinned. "Oh," he said, "hey, that's pretty funny ...."

And that cracked them up all over again, sending them into the roaring sort of contagious laughter that you can't stop until it simply hurts too much to keep on laughing.

At that precise instant there was an explosion near the front of the bus, not a big flash and bang, blow-your-hair-off sort of an explosion, but a definite explosive event, which produced a huge puff of black smoke and a panic stricken bus driver, who pulled the bus to the side of the road, slammed on the brakes, shut off the engine, and threw open the door.

"Everybody out of the bus! Out of the bus! Women and children first!" he shouted as he jumped off the bus first.

Had he used a calmer, more user-friendly tone, perhaps there would not have been such a panic. On the other hand, Damon had spent his life riding school buses, and not a day went by when he didn't wonder what it would be like to throw open the emergency door. He jerked the big handle downward. "Out the back!" he shouted, and then rushed forward to get the smaller kids moving in the right direction.

"Hey!" he shouted to the soccer players. "Catch the little kids. It's too far to jump."

Meanwhile the smoke had grown considerably thicker and blacker, and he could hear someone mumbling and grumbling.

"Whoever that is, get off the bus!" he shouted. He got down on his hands and knees and started forward, keeping below the smoke, which now was rushing out of the bus at both ends, making it look like an enormous double-ended yellow barbecue. But there was something weird about this smoke. Once outside it rose no higher than about ten feet. As soon as it escaped the bus it just hung in the air in a black, thick blanket.

"Who's in there? Is anybody in there?"

No answer. He continued crawling, looking for feet and legs dangling from the seats. It paid off. "Com'on," he said to the three kids huddled in the seat, "crawl under the smoke."

They climbed down and began crawling rapidly toward the front of the bus. He found two more kids, and then checked each seat until he reached the front of the bus, making sure everyone was out, before he crawled back under the smoke to the middle of the bus, took a deep breath, stood, opened several windows, dropped to the floor, took another deep breath, and opened several more windows.

As the smoke began to clear, there, standing in the middle of the bus, was Larry the Rat, wearing a white lab coat, a beat-up baseball cap that said "Chemistry Rules," and holding a large jug. He looked at Damon and then down at the jug. "Damn stuff is extremely unstable," he said. "Just the bouncing of the bus set it off."

"Maybe you better get it outside before it blows up," Damon said, looking uneasily at the jug.

"It won't blow up. It can't blow up. It isn't explosive. It was the pressure from the chemicals. I got the mix wrong again." He shook his head and looked down at the jug, which had suddenly stopped smoking. "This is the trickiest compound I ever synthesized," he said. "But at least now I know it doesn't like being shaken." The air had cleared, and Larry reached down, picked a cork off the seat and twisted it back into the top of the bottle.

"Wait! Won't that make it go off again?" Damon asked.

"Naw. Once it's over it's over. It uses up all the chemical that catalyzes the reaction and that's that." He sat down in his seat. "You can tell 'em it's okay," he said.

Damon laughed. "You think anyone is going to get back on the bus while that jug is still here?"

"I told you it's safe."

At that moment three policemen leaped into the back of the bus while a fire crew came in from the front.

"Clear the bus! Everyone clear the bus!" The first fireman shouted as he rushed toward them, extinguisher at the ready.

Damon and Larry stood their ground.

"Where's the fire? Where's the fire?" the second fireman shouted.

"Hey! Get off the bus," one of the policemen shouted.

"There's no fire," Damon said.

All five men stared at him, their brains cranking slowly through what they knew. The way they saw it, where there's smoke, there's fire.

"Then what caused all the smoke?" one fireman asked.

Larry held up the jug and the men recoiled as if it were a bomb. "My chemistry experiment," he said. "I didn't get the mixture right, and it built up some pressure and blew the cork out of the jug. It's over and I put the cork back in."

Skeptical. Very skeptical. The cops rubbed their chins and the firemen removed their masks. Then the largest of the three policemen stepped forward. "You're telling us you brought a bomb onto a school bus?"

"It's not a bomb," Larry said. "There's nothing in this that could explode."

"But what if the cork had been too tight and the pressure built up and sent pieces of glass flying everywhere?" The policeman, whose name tag read Snapper, had clearly decided, as he worked things out, that what he had here was a bomb. He turned to the man behind him. "Better get the bomb squad down here," he said. Then he turned and waved his arms. "Okay. We got a bomb situation here! Put the jug down, son, and back away from it there ... everybody get clear! Move those people outside away from the bus there!"

"It's not a bomb!" Larry insisted.

The cop was having none of it and he reached for his pistol. "I told you to put the jug down and back away!" he shouted.

Damon began to back away, his eyes wide as he tried to figure out how this thing had gotten so far out of hand so fast. "Hey, hold it," he said. He held out his hands palms forward as he backed away, his eyes focused on Snapper's hand hovering just above the grips of his pistol. "We aren't criminals! We're just kids!"

Larry looked at the cop, then down at the jug, and then in a flash, tossed the bottle through the open window.

What followed was a lot of screaming and running around, with cops and firemen and kids running for cover as the jug sailed in a shallow arc out the window and broke into a thousand pieces on the sidewalk. And nothing happened except that the liquid in the bottle ran off into the storm drain.

Larry shook his head. "It wasn't a bomb," he said.

But Snapper simply shifted gears. "Cancel the bomb squad and get the chemical pollution squad down here on the double. We got us a superfund incident!"

Larry walked to the front of the bus and climbed down with Damon and everyone else following him. He walked over, dipped his finger in the remaining liquid, and stuck his finger into his mouth. "This is perfectly harmless stuff," he said. "Once it's exposed to air it goes into a stabilization reaction which reduces the chemicals to oxygen, carbon and hydrogen, and ..."

"Hydrogen!" Snapper hollered. "Stay back, it's hydrogen! We got us a madman here with a hydrogen bomb!"

People began running wildly, some of them screaming as they ran.

DISCARD

NLSP HIGH SCHOOL LIBRARY

30301

Again Larry shook his head. "The same stuff you're breathing," he said, showing not the least sign of irritation.

Now there were sirens howling everywhere.

"You're under arrest, young man!" Snapper shouted. "Read him his rights!"

Just then another man walked up. He was younger and dressed in a dark suit. "What's going on here?"

Snapper turned. "I'm arresting this madman, Chief!"

"What for?"

"Transporting an illegal and dangerous device of a chemical nature."

"What sort of device?"

Snapper stabbed his arm out, pointing at the broken jug. "Right there, Chief!"

The chief, a man much given to facts, held up his hands with the palms forward. "Before we make an arrest, maybe we ought to find out whether it was a dangerous device."

"Oh, there's no question of that, Chief," Snapper said. "All these witnesses heard him say that it was hydrogen!"

"And oxygen and carbon," Larry said. "When the mixture is exposed to air it reverts to the basic organic elements." He shrugged, "But first it tends to give off a little smoke."

The chief nodded.

"There, he said it again! Smoke! You got smoke, you got trouble," Snapper said.

The chief shook his head slowly. "Well," he said in a tone that dripped sarcasm, "I think before we clap this young lad in irons and draw up a list of particulars for the next assizes, we'll have the substance tested to see whether it was in the least way dangerous."

He turned to Larry. "Just what did it start out as?"

"Can't tell you," Larry said.

"Because you don't know?"

"It's a secret formula."

The chief nodded again. "And what will we find when we have it analyzed?"

"Oxygen, carbon, and hydrogen."

"Is there any danger in breathing the smoke?"

"There's nothing toxic in the smoke. All the chemicals I used, even in combination with each other are nontoxic."

Mr. Waters appeared from nowhere. "Hey there, Henry," he said as he came up behind the police chief, "What have we got? Another of Larry's experiments acting up?"

"Hey, Harmon, how's it going?"

Mr. Waters shrugged. "The usual."

"I take it this has happened before?"

"Nearly every time he gets to the chem lab."

"Nothing dangerous?"

Mr. Waters shook his head. "Tom Potter says it's harmless, and that's good enough for me."

"Me too," Henry said. "Best science teacher I ever had."

"I'm sorry about all this," Larry said. He looked truly embarrassed.

"Tom tells me," Mr. Waters said, "that Larry is the school genius, at least in science." He grinned. "He could stand to put in a little more time in history, though. Only had a ninety-five average this week. Every other grade was a hundred."

Larry looked even more embarrassed. He shrugged, stuffing his hands into his pockets as he looked up at the two men. "Everybody's dead," he said.

"What?" Henry looked up quickly.

"In history ... they're all dead. Very boring."

Both men laughed.

Mr. Waters turned to the kids. "Okay, everybody back on the bus," he called.

Slowly the kids returned and began climbing onto the bus as Damon dropped into the seat next to Larry. "You okay?" he asked.

"Sure. Fine." He glanced furtively at Damon. "I think that cop is totally nuts, you know that?"

"For a second I thought he was gonna pull his gun and shoot us."

"Boy, talk about weird!" He turned in his seat and looked carefully at Damon. "That was pretty quick thinking, the way you got everybody off the bus."

"I'm a quarterback. What I do is give orders."

"I could never do something like that."

"Sure you could. All it takes is practice. Thirty-six, fifty-two, hike ... hike ... hike..." He grinned. "See, practice. And as long as everyone knows what the numbers mean, it works."

Larry looked fully around at him, his eyebrows arched. "You mean all the players have to know that?"

"Sure. It's a code that tells them what play we're going to run, and where they have to go, and what they have to do to make the play work."

"Football players can remember all that?"

"And a lot more. When I come up to the line I have to know how to read the defense so I can change the play if the other team is set up so the play I called won't work."

"And you use a different set of codes."

"You catch on quick."

"Talk about having the wrong idea ... I thought all you did was go out there and bang into each other 'til the only one standing was the guy with the ball." He pulled the brim of his cap down toward his nose. "I got a lot to learn," he said.

"Tell you what. I'll teach you about football, if, when I have to take chemistry, you'll help me with that." He looked down. "I mean, that is if you want to learn about football."

"Okay," Larry said. "It'd make my dad happy if I'd sit and watch some games with him. He really likes football."

"Hey, it's a great game."

"Doesn't it hurt when you get hit?"

"Most of the time you just shake it off."

"Why would you do that? Why would you play a game where you got hurt all the time?"

"Because on the football field you can get to be a hero."

"Hero?"

"Yeah."

"And heroes are something good?"

"I don't know about that, but I do know that some very pretty girls seem to like football players."

"That's why you do it?"

"No, well, sure, some of it, I suppose."

"Then why else?"

He didn't know why else. He had never thought about it. You just played football because it was football. "You sure ask a lot of questions," Damon said.

"That's how I learn stuff."

"Okay, I got a question for you. How come you wear your hat with the brim facing forward?"

"To shade my eyes. That's why you have a brim on a cap. What good does it do to wear it shading your neck?"

"Cool. It's cool and you gotta be cool, right?"

"Why? I mean, if you have to let someone else make the rules about the way you behave, why would you want to be cool? Why let someone else tell you what to do?"

Again, he had no answer. He wasn't even sure he wanted to think about it, but worst of all, now that he *was* thinking about it, he was gonna think about it more, and that would only lead to confusion. A quarterback had to keep a clear head. No confusion. Think about the ball .

"Besides, with a nose as big as mine," Larry said, "if I wore my hat backwards nobody would know whether I was coming or going."

Damon laughed, deciding as he looked at Larry the Rat, that he liked this guy. He might be a genius, and a book worm, and weird looking, but he was also funny and smart. There was no way you could tell what he was gonna say next, and you had to admire someone like that.

Damon leaned in close. "Just what was that stuff?" he asked in a whisper.

"Can't tell you."

"I mean, I know what you told the cops and all, but what was it really? Was it dangerous?"

"It's a secret. I can't say anything until I get it worked out and patented. But you don't have to worry. It isn't dangerous at all. I used to do stuff like that, but my dad made me quit before I blew up the house."

"You can make bombs and stuff?"

"Any little kid with a chemistry set and access to the Internet can do that. I'm talking serious chemistry here." He sounded hurt.

"Hey, sorry, I didn't mean to, you know, to imply that you were doing something weird."

"The way I see it, football is lot more weird than anything that happens in chemistry."

"Hey, I said I was sorry."

Larry looked around and grinned. "No," he said. "I'm sorry. Bad habit. I got a terrible thin skin when it comes to anything that even sounds like an insult."

Damon grinned back. "It's okay," he said. "I shouldn't have been so nosey. That's my problem." But now another thought had crept in. He remembered the way Larry walked and moved, and there was nothing the least uncoordinated about him. In fact, he was quick and smooth as a weasel, and that didn't fit a guy who was a lab rat. More like a gym rat.

Chapter Four

Negotiating With the Bear

When your father has been a Marine and a star football player in high school, and when he is a master mechanic who can fix any engine, even the new ones with their fancy computers, he ought to be predictable. But Harley Foxrucker was not a predictable man. On the other hand, his father had named him for a motorcycle, so whimsey had, in the Foxrucker clan, been built on a solid foundation.

Grandpa Charlie Foxrucker still rode a big Harley, and it was surely an odd sight when he came gliding up with the motorcycle grumbling and growling like an irritated lion. How many grandfathers ran around in full leather outfits, wore their hair in a pony tail, and carried a switchblade? Nobody but his. And Gramma Jean wasn't much different. She wore leathers too, and she bleached her hair and ... she was, when you came right down to it, a babe.

None of this sat well with Damon's mother, who came from a college-educated family where grandmothers looked like ... grandmothers. The men in her family worked in offices, and they had sailboats, and when something needed to be repaired, they hired someone. Family gatherings, as a result, were somewhat strained. Dad's side drank beer, Mom's side went with white wine. And yet, he'd noticed that the men on both sides seemed to have plenty of respect for each other. The women, however, barely spoke.

As he walked along the narrow road to his house in the least populated section of town, Damon wondered why they acted that way. What was the point? All it did was make things unpleasant. Why, if the men could always find something to talk about, couldn't the women find something to talk about?

Clearly, he had a lot to learn. He shook his head, wondering if you ever did learn stuff like that. Maybe it was best not to think about it, because the more you thought about it, the more confused you got, and right now he did not need any more confusion. He needed to get his thinking running in a straight line, so when he approached Dad with his idea to run a private practice on Sundays, he would buy into it. That would not be easy. It was like proposing a revolution.

He opened the door of the old farmhouse and walked in, dropping his book bag in the front hall, before heading for the kitchen and the refrigerator. Food. He needed food. He always lots and lots of food, especially meat and milk and apple pie.

Damon looked over at the big schoolhouse clock as he set a ham on the counter and got out a knife. They wouldn't eat till seven, and that was still two hours away. Mom got home at six and Dad came in from the shop at six-thirty, which gave Damon time to eat and get most of his homework out of the way. And Belle was at their cousin's house, where she went every day, which meant the house was absolutely quiet.

He slapped the ham onto a big slice of rye bread covered with mayonnaise, added more ham, and finally some lettuce. That would hold him for awhile, he thought, as he put the ham away, poured a glass of milk, and sat at the booth by the big bay window that looked out over what once had been a farm. It had been taken over by junk cars. For a month every summer he took cars apart and put the parts in the bins in the barn. It was as endless as the jobs those guys in mythology got. As fast as he took the cars apart, more showed up. But the truth was, he didn't mind that. After all, Dad paid him ten bucks an hour, and he could use any of the parts he wanted, which was how he'd put together his own monster truck. And they had dirt roads everywhere, so he drove all the time, and not many guys had a deal like that.

And living where they did, where farm country took over from the town, not only provided them with the space to do what they wanted, but it allowed them to play fast and loose with the zoning laws about junk vehicles. The best thing, though, was that he was getting to play football.

Foxruckers played football, then they went into the Marines. Football was great, but he wasn't so sure about the Marines. He was thinking more along the lines of college, because that way he'd get to play football for at least eight years, and the more time you spent playing sports, the less time you spent worrying about who was dating who and why girls acted so weird. And, of course you could keep on dreaming too, dreaming about maybe one day playing for the Packers.

But for now, football kept things simple. Wrestling in the winter and track in the spring rounded out the year. Play sports, go out on dates and stay away from all the gossip and confusion. And get good grades. You had to get good grades if you wanted to choose a college instead of the college choosing you. And you had to get better than the C's he'd been getting. He needed B's and A's. He sighed, carried his plate and glass to the sink, rinsed them off and put them in the dishwasher. At least he had one A ... in math, but only because algebra was so easy. He hauled his backpack upstairs to his room, sat at his desk by the window, turned on the light, and took out his algebra book, deciding to do the easy stuff first. Science and math were easy. They made sense. History was another matter. The book put him to sleep. English was okay, because at least the stories were interesting, but you could never be sure you got anything right.

And tonight he had to write an essay, which meant he was probably not gonna do too well on it, because once again he'd put it off 'til the night before. Write. Write about what? A personal experience. He couldn't think of anything. Well, he could, like the time he and Sissy Williams had ... but you couldn't write about stuff like that. He grinned ... you put anything like that on paper and you'd be in jail. Besides, it had to be something important to impress the teacher, and that left him with nothing to write about, because he didn't think Miss Carstairs would be much impressed by anything he'd done.

He opened the algebra book. First things first.

Belle, even if she was his sister, and even if she was only ten, was a pretty girl, and he could see she was gonna break a lot of hearts. But the best thing about Belle was that she never ratted him out. No matter what she knew about what he did, she never went to Mom with anything.

But at dinner she started the conversation off with a stunner. "I heard some kid blew up the school bus," she said.

"What!" Grace Foxrucker whirled toward her daughter.

"No, it was nothing like that" Damon said. "This kid had his chemistry experiment with him, and it suddenly started smoking, that's all."

"Isn't that kind of dangerous? Taking a chemistry experiment on the bus?" Grace looked over at her husband, but if he had heard any of the conversation he showed no sign. He was applying himself to his roast beef with particular vigor.

"Not with this kid, Mom," Damon said. "He's a genius. He

said he just didn't get the mixture right."

"Was it scary?" Belle asked.

"Yeah, at first. Especially making sure all the kids got off the bus in the smoke. But it was cool too. I got to open the emergency door."

Harley looked up. "I heard the call on the radio. That screwball Eddie Snapper called for the bomb squad. How that guy ever got to be a cop, I'll never know. He was dumb in high school and I think he's gotten dumber."

"Kind of like our coach," Damon said.

"What's wrong with old Bunker?"

"He only uses running plays."

"You win a lot of football games running the ball."

"I'm a quarterback, Dad, remember?"

"Lots of quarterbacks run the ball."

"Dad, there's no future in being a quarterback if you don't get to throw, and you know how well I can throw."

He set his fork down and scowled, his thick eyebrows and dark eyes making him look fierce as a bear wakened from hibernation. "Quit grousing and do what the coach tells you."

"Why should I listen to a coach who hasn't won a game in four years."

"Four years!"

"He's won just eight games in seven years."

The scowl was gone. "Guess I kinda lost track." He shook his head. "Wonder what happened to old Bunker. He used to be a good coach, I thought."

"Only when some kid turned up who could run."

"Seems to me I remember Phil and Charlie saying something about that." He shrugged. "Oh well, he's the coach."

"Please don't shrug, dear," Grace said.

He set his fork down. "What's everybody in your family got against shrugging?"

"It's not polite."

Damon was not about to let the conversation drift. "I had this idea, Dad, that maybe if I got some of the guys together on the weekend, you could help us work out some pass patterns and get the timing down."

Harley looked carefully at his son, weighing what he was up to. It didn't seem too complicated. "And then if you get into a game you'll cut loose one of those plays."

"Right."

"And then Bunker'll bench you for the season."

"Maybe not. I think Mr. Waters would see it my way."

He picked up his fork. "Good man, Harmon Waters. Marine right to the core." He speared a piece of beef. "What makes you think he'd be on your side?"

"I can talk to him."

Grace picked up on that very quickly. "How is it you are getting to know the principal?"

"Uh, no particular reason."

"You've been sent to the office?" Harley asked.

"Sure." He shrugged.

"Don't shrug, dear," Grace said.

"Why are you getting sent to the office?" Harley asked.

"Big mouth."

Harley grinned at his wife. "Well, he didn't get that from my side of the family."

"It's okay, Mom. He just laughs and we work things out. He's a really good guy. As long as you're straight with him, he's straight with you."

"He played baseball in college," Harley said. "Down at the state university. He was a heck of a hitter. Made second team All-American."

"Why didn't he go pro?"

"He could have, the Phillies picked him in the draft, but he went into the Marines because of the war. He wanted to get it out of the way so he could go to graduate school. Harmon and I go back a long, long way."

"Will you help us out?"

"How many guys you got?"

"The center and the receivers."

"How many pass plays you got in your book?"

"Four."

"That's all?"

"All of 'em are Hail Marys."

"You gotta throw the ball once in a while or the running game won't work."

Suddenly Belle chimed in. "Marjorie Simmons says her sister's in love with you."

"What?"

"Do you know her?"

"Yeah, sure. I know her."

"She's really pretty, isn't she?"

Thin ice. Very thin ice. "Yup."

"Do you like her?"

"Sure," he said, trying to make it sound casual.

"You should ask her out."

"I only just met her, Belle."

"She's very nice," Belle said. "She's even nice to her little sister, which is more than I can say for some siblings."

Harley laughed, a great booming sound. "Where in heck did you learn that word?"

"Television. I learn a lot of things from television."

Harley grunted. The only thing he watched on television was sports. The rest of what came over the TV was junk.

Again Damon retargeted the conversation. "I think if I got into a game and I ran a pass play and we scored or made a big gain, then Bunker would have to use more pass plays. But without some practice, that won't happen."

"What time would you want to get these guys together?" Harley asked.

"One o'clock on Sunday. I thought we'd meet at the park."

"Okay. At one. You got any plays in mind?"

"A couple of flares, post patterns, maybe a curl."

He nodded. "Easy enough. Out of a pro set?"

"Too obvious. From the option T."

"I'll draw some up and we'll see how it goes." He shook his head. "I don't like this much, going against the coach."

"It's not just me, Dad, we got a wide receiver who can run like the wind, and his friends say he can catch anything."

"Has Bunker ever played a freshman before?"

"Only in an emergency."

"What's going to cause that?"

"Second-string quarterback tripped over the bench and tore up his knee, and the first string guy's afraid of getting hit."

His father nodded. "What's your guess, two games?"

He shrugged. "Maybe three. He's gonna get hit just as he turns away from the play, and he'll never see it coming."

"Don't shrug, dear," Grace said.

"Be sure to say hi to Jenny for me," Belle said.

He could feel himself getting hot. "I hardly ever see her."

But his mother and sister both noticed the way his face had changed color, and they grinned at each other. Football might be something as foreign as pancakes covered with chicken gravy, but boyfriends and girlfriends they understood.

"I think you like her," Belle said.

"I don't even know her."

"Do you think she's pretty?"

"Give it a rest will you, Belle?"

"Just tell me."

"So you can report back to Marjorie? Not a chance. I may be a boy, but that doesn't mean I'm dumb." He grinned. "And I don't come from Mars either."

Chapter Five

Out of the Rathole

Okay, so he looked like a rat, he knew that, and there was nothing he could do except try to forget it. Not so easy. Girls don't date rats or smart guys. They date football players like Damon, and guys like that don't have anything to do with rats, either the lab type or the Norway brown types.

Larry turned on the Bunsen burner beneath his latest concoction, adjusted the flame so it would cook more slowly, and then picked up his thoughts where he had left them.

On the other hand, Damon had not only talked to him, he had defended him, and maybe he was different. He shook his head. Don't bet on it. Hanging out with me would wreck his reputation, and nobody messed with that. You had to be cool, even if the whole idea of being cool was idiotic.

He looked around the large basement room he had built in the ranch house where he lived with his parents and his two little brothers. The door had a lock, and he had his own computer and phone and fax, and until today he had been perfectly happy down here. It was quiet and his brothers couldn't get at him. Brothers? Sometimes he thought they must've had different parents. They were interested in sports, and he had never liked sports. But there was a reason. Somebody hit a baseball, it caught him in the nose. Somebody passed a basketball, it hit him in the nose. And football ... no matter what you did in football, it hurt. But the worst part was all the crap he'd had to take. And for most of his life he'd had no choice. He hadn't been strong enough to get into a fight without getting the dust kicked out of him. But that was different now, because now he had a third degree black belt. Oddly, that had made fighting pointless.

He watched the liquid begin to boil, and then set the timer, certain he'd get it right this time. But with something new you could never be sure. A lot of it was trial and error. He grinned. Kind of like his life, only in reverse — mostly error and then trial. Not that there weren't rewards. He had a straight A average and that would pay off in two years when he picked a college. Then he'd have the last laugh. Wrong. He'd go to college and turn into a lab rat with a white coat, and the only girls he'd meet would be lab rats too. He wanted to date a cheerleader or some girl who was really, really hot. What he wanted was to be part of the ordinary, normal world, but that didn't happen to a guy who was still only five-five and looked like a rat. How come he wasn't getting any bigger? His father was five-ten, Mom was five-six. Nobody on either side of the family was short.

He picked the beaker from the heat and carefully poured in chemicals to catalyze the reaction. When the black oily smoke began to pour from the beaker, he sighed, turned on the exhaust fan, and walked back to the lab bench. He snuffed out the reaction with water, and marked the failure in his notebook. Then, anticipating what was coming, he got up and walked to the door, opening it just as his father arrived.

"Larry! What the hell's going on down here?"

"Nothing, now."

His father peered through the thin gray haze. "I thought

you'd set the place on fire."

"No, it's okay, Dad."

His father, blinked. "Yeah, well it sure doesn't look okay."

"Just a test run."

"Huh." He looked decidedly skeptical. But then he usually looked that way in matters of chemistry, which he lumped into the same category as black magic. "Just be careful, will you? Your mother nearly had a heart attack when she saw all that smoke."

"Okay."

"Oh, and you had a phone call. Some kid named Damon Fox-something. Wants you to call him back."

"Damon Foxrucker? And he wants me to call him back?"

"His number is upstairs. And it's nearly time for bed."

"I'll have to call Damon first." He dashed up the stairs and into the kitchen, found the number on the notebook by the phone, and punched it into the key pad.

A girl answered.

"Hello," he said, "this is Larry Perkins, is Damon there?"

"Just a minute, please."

He waited for what seemed like a long time, and the longer he waited, the more his nerves began working on him. By the time Damon answered, his knees were shaking.

"Hi, Larry, how you doin'? Sorry, I was taking a leak."

"No problem," Larry said, trying to sound as if guys said things like that to him all the time. Hey, just one of the gang.

"We're getting together Sunday at one to work some plays," Damon said, "I thought it'd be a good time to start learning."

"Sure, where?"

"At the park. Do you need a ride?"

"I can get there." He hesitated, trying to remember the family schedule. John had a guitar lesson at one-thirty and Harry had soccer practice. That meant he'd have to ride his bike, and nobody rode bikes, but what difference would that make? He was already at the top of the geek charts. "I won't have to like ...

play or anything will I? Cause I'm pretty bad at sports."

"Naw, just watch and I'll explain what's going on."

"Okay. I'll be there."

"Good. See you then."

He hung up the phone, and for the first time in a long while he smiled, not his usual ironic grin, but just a great big, absolutely happy sort of smile. Maybe his life was gonna take a turn for the better. Maybe.... He shook his head. No. This would last for awhile, and then he'd be back into his old rut. The question was how to keep that from happening? Tough question. Were you stuck with the personality you had, or could you make changes? From a scientific point of view, he thought you were stuck, but when you factored in hopes and wishes, it was clear that you could make changes. One thing he knew, absolutely. He was going to give it his best.

The park was five miles away, a nothing ride on his bike. Larry could flat-out fly, the big Cannondale racer just a slashing flash of silver in the warm September afternoon. He wore a helmet, goggles, yellow and blue skin-tight shorts, and shirt to match. Until now this had served as a disguise.

He was used to thirty miles. A five-mile run was a sprint, and he treated it that way, flying down the streets, his head almost on the handle bars to offer as little resistance to the wind as possible. It was not play. This summer he was going to enter every race he could find. And when he turned nineteen, he planned to take a shot at the Olympic team. What he had facing him until then was the Nautilus and his bike.

He came into the park at full speed and headed for the playing field where the small knot of guys in shorts and gray tee-shirts stood facing a man who looked as wide as a bear. He slowed as he came up onto the grass and braked to a stop.

Nobody knew who he was. All they saw was a short guy, who had very long legs, corded with muscle that looked as hard as iron. Larry leaned his bike against one of the green park benches and took off his helmet.

"Sorry I'm late," he said.

Damon grinned and walked over to look at the bike. "That is an awesome bike," he said. "You race?"

"This summer. I'm just training now."

Damon grinned. "And I thought you were just a lab geek." He slapped him on the shoulder. "That is pure California."

Larry smiled. "Bike racing doesn't get much space on the sports pages," he said.

Damon's dad had squatted down, looking over the gears and the shifting system on the bike, and Damon knew he was impressed with what he saw.

"Larry, this is my Dad," Damon said, as his father stood.

Larry reached out to shake hands and watched his own hand disappear in a bear-sized paw. "Nice to meet you, sir."

"Same here, Larry." He nodded toward the bike. "Nice piece of equipment."

"Thank you, sir."

"You're not a football player, are you?"

"This is the guy I told you about, Dad. He just wants to find out something about football." Damon turned toward the other players. "Guys, this is Larry Perkins, a friend of mine."

They nodded, but they were clearly wary.

Harley nodded. "Well, let's get going." He turned toward the players. "We'll start with the post pattern I outlined."

Damon stepped in over Joe Santos, the center, called the signals, and on the snap Warren Wilson and Roger Wilkes took off straight down the field, while Melvin held in blocking position. Warren made his cut first, pivoting on his inside foot and slanting toward the middle of the field while Roger went straight. Damon dropped back, pumped the ball once and let it fly.

Larry thought he had never seen anyone run so fast. They were like streaks of light, but the biggest surprise came when Damon fired the football in a perfect spiral right into Warren's outstretched hands. I may not know much about football, Larry thought, but I think that was a long way from normal.

Warren trotted back and tossed Damon the ball. "You said you could throw, Foxrucker, and I guess you can! I never caught a football moving that fast, and I was thirty yards away!"

Harley grinned. A natural born wide receiver. It was more than you could hope for. And then it got better, because Roger Wilkes, while not as fast as Warren, had great big, soft hands and he caught anything that came near him. And Melvin Upshaw for all his size, had quick feet and soft hands.

They ran little flare passes toward the sidelines over and over, and then they ran curls, the receiver running full speed upfield, suddenly stopping and stepping back toward the quarterback. The trick was to have the ball and the player arrive at the same spot at the same instant.

Sometimes that happened, but most often it didn't, and the ball sailed just past the receiver's fingertips, or it went behind just enough to make the catch impossible. After one particularly wide miss, Harley shouted, "Damon! Remember all the skeet you shot. Remember to lead!"

Damon took the next snap, backpeddled, stepped up, and in his mind he pictured the clay disks flying out from the skeet thrower. He cocked his arm, picked a point well ahead of Warren and threw. The ball came down right on Warren's hands, and he caught it without having to slow or change direction.

It was something you did the first time by thinking about it, and then, as you fell into a rhythm, you did it by instinct, knowing how fast your receiver was running, and when he'd get to the ball. The post pattern worked every time. For some reason, with the receiver going away, he could just unload, and all the receiver had to do was pluck the ball out of the air.

The short passes, the flares, gave him the most trouble, but then, as he thought about it, so did the clay pigeons on the skeet range when he had to shoot toward the corners. They took a break after an hour, sitting on the grass as Mr. Foxrucker explained how to fake by using your head or your shoulders to get open. All you needed was a half step to get clear.

The other parents had arrived early and they stood out of the way, watching their sons perform. Across the park, perhaps fifty yards away, an older model Chevy pickup sat by the curb, the large man inside watching the practice with great intensity. Two things caught and held Coach Bunker's attention. The first was Harley Foxrucker. A running back. Maybe the best running back he'd ever seen, including a lot of the guys in the pros. Four years in a row Walley's Falls had won the state championship with Foxrucker at tailback. He should have been schooling running backs, but instead he was teaching them the passing game. The second thing that caught his eye was Damon Foxrucker. He had an arm. A real arm. He threw perfect spirals and they were accurate and fast and ... he shook his head and placed both hands on the steering wheel. There was Harley Foxrucker, a pure running back, out there showing them how to run pass patterns. Maybe it was only because he had a son who could throw, but wouldn't he have done the same if he'd had a son like that? He started the truck. Well, at least he knew what was coming.

After each play Harley explained why he hadn't gone for the fake. Roger Wilkes caught on first. Without Warren's speed, he had to use every fake he could imagine. But it turned out that he needed only half a step because when he got those big, soft hands near the ball he made the catch.

The excitement was contagious and soon the parents were cheering each play. It is always exciting to see a skill emerge for the first time, to see it suddenly appear as if by magic, and they could hardly stand still. The fathers understood the instant it appeared, because they had played sports, and they knew when the play moved to another level. The mothers knew more by instinct, judging the improvement by the carriage of the young men on the field. They walked taller, their strides confident and self-assured, more like men than boys.

Larry saw it in vastly different terms. It was an exercise in flying geometry and physics. It was the laws of Sir Isaac Newton practically applied, and he found it exciting, even thinking he might like to try it, until he heard Mr. Foxrucker describe what happens to receivers when they catch the ball. They get hit. Hard. They are vulnerable because they have to focus on the ball instead of the defensive man, who, because he let the guy catch the ball, has a strong interest in making him pay.

What nobody saw was the older, somewhat battered green Chevy pickup drive off.

After practice he stood next to his bike.

"Well, did you learn anything?" Damon asked.

Larry nodded. "How can you throw a football like that?"

Damon held up the ball in one hand. "Big mitts," he said. His fingers reached better than halfway around the ball. He grinned. "I've also got a lot of football players in the family, so I get coached all the time."

Larry watched him carefully. Nobody liked being told how to do anything, especially not kids. But obviously Damon had listened, and he'd let people coach him, and usually the big guys were the last to listen, particularly football players, who were so full of themselves it was a wonder they didn't explode like seed pods in a hot fall sun. "You did that?"

"What?"

"I mean, you, let them tell you what to do?"

Damon shrugged. "Proof's in the pudding, Larry. Did you see my old man out there? When he was defending, nobody caught a pass. He was a running back. Never played defense. Maybe it's just easier to listen when the guy who's telling you can do it better than you can."

Larry was stunned. How come a football player understood that? Not even smart kids understood stuff like that, or if they did, they refused to admit it. I know, he thought, but only because my bike coach, even at fifty-three, can fly down the road like he's got a motor doing the work instead of just his legs and some advantageous gear ratios.

"I've been meaning to ask you," Damon said, "You've got your license, right?"

"Yeah."

"You going to the prom?"

"What?" It was truly not a question he had considered.

"The prom? Are you going?"

"Rats do not go to proms."

Damon laughed.

"What's funny about that?"

"Maybe you oughta ask somebody."

"You're suggesting a double date?"

"Yeah, is that so weird?"

"Maybe."

"Because I can't drive?"

"Yeah. I mean, like, you need a ride, right?"

"Sure."

"Why me? I mean, why not somebody from the team?"

"I see those guys all the time."

"You're really serious, aren't you."

"Yeah."

Larry shook his head, trying to fight past the suspicion that he was somehow being used. Logically, the only reason Damon would get into this was because he needed a ride. But that presumed Damon was like other people, and he already knew that was a long way from true.

"Look," Damon said, "all you need is a date."

"No girl will go out with me," Larry said.

"How many have you asked?"

"Hey, some things you just know."

Damon shrugged. "Everybody gets turned down. You just have to keep asking."

"Have you got a date?"

"Not yet."

"But you know who you're gonna ask."

"Sure."

"What if she says no?"

"Then I ask someone else."

"Doesn't that bother you?"

"Yeah."

"But you do it anyway?"

He shrugged. "I want to go to the prom, that's all."

Larry laughed. "I'll think about it," he said.

"Damon!" Harley called. "Light a fire under it!"

"Gotta go," Damon said. "See you here tomorrow?"

"Sure. What time?"

"After practice," Damon said.

He took the long, long, long way home, deciding that in as much as he was out, he might as well get in some work. Thirty miles of work and thirty miles of thinking. Could it possibly be true that all the stereotypes about football players had no basis in truth? Weren't they supposed to be rock-headed, totally physical jocks? Bullies? Or was it just Damon? No, it was more than Damon, because the other guys out there had been able to take instruction and apply what they were told. So maybe it was just those guys? What about the other players?

The question produced an uneasiness. There was trouble ahead. He could smell it as surely as he could tell from the gasses that came off his chemistry experiments what chemicals he had used. He felt as if he were watching two trains coming down a track toward each other at high speed. What bothered him was that just now he could only identify one of the trains.

Chapter Six

The Rumble Brothers

Richie Barber, Kyle Pettibone, and Keith Jones called themselves the Rumble Brothers. They were the tough guys with a reputation for fighting. They drove sleek street rods, stopping at the hangouts: the McDonald's parking lot, Louie's Pizza, Clinton's Shell, and anywhere else where kids might gather. Except the mall. They'd been banned because of the fight they'd started there with a bunch of guys from Bridgeton.

All of their fights were with tough guys from out of town, but they never got into fights with football or hockey players, because those guys were crazy. It was like they couldn't feel any pain. Finally, they ran out of guys to fight. Out-of-town guys didn't go to Wally's Falls anymore, and the Rumble Brothers did not court trouble on another man's turf. But a life without thrills is no life at all, and they started looking elsewhere to salve the alcohol-frayed ends of their minds.

They turned to pot, and because there wasn't enough kick from just smoking it, they began selling it. Then they began carrying guns in addition to the knives they had always carried.

Nobody checked them. Nobody paid any attention. Not only was Wally's Falls a peaceful town, but most of the parents came from a generation where everybody smoked pot, and they saw no harm in 'recreational' drugs. People seldom see the harm in what makes them feel good, though those are usually the very things that cause harm.

But something else had changed in Wally's Falls. It was a very different town from what it had been when the mills were running. Then it had been home to a rowdy crowd, grown men, who spent a good part of every paycheck in the saloons to escape their dreary jobs. The mills were dark and noisy, the chemical-heavy air acid and rank from the molten brass. It shortened their lives, even as it killed the trees on the hills which framed the narrow valley. For a long, long time no one could explain why the trees died.

For three generations the only escape had been to go to war. It gave the young men a way to leave, to taste adventure, and danger, before they drifted back, got married, and raised a family. Some never returned. Those who died got their names carved into the polished granite slabs in front of the town hall, and on Memorial Day the American Legion set flags by their stones in the graveyards. Some escaped by simply drifting, looking for a way to avoid a lifetime in the mills.

Now those mills were closed, the big stone and brick buildings standing empty, most of the windows boarded over. A lot of the old company row housing had been torn down to make way for stores and small parks. Subdivisions had sprung up on what once had been farmland surrounding the small central city. It had become a suburban community, located within easy commute of two big cities. The crime rate was nonexistent. The trees had begun to grow back. Some of the old mills were converted to factory outlet stores. The result was a social vacuum which buffered them from the nastiness of the outside world.

Meanwhile the Rumble Brothers built a drug business. They

operated out of an abandoned mill building. They sold their street rods, because they were too visible, and replaced them with common sorts of cars in dark blue or black. It was not that they were so smart as shrewd. They wore no gang colors, but dressed like everyone else, effecting a kind of camouflage. Their customers understood the change, but to the police, to their parents, to their teachers, and to the administrators at the school, it looked as if they had simply begun to grow up. Business flourished. They sold only pot and they built substantial bank accounts.

But greed recognizes no limits. The way their supplier saw it, the territory wasn't being tapped. So Angelo Stompenado paid them a visit. Keith, Kyle, and Richie met him at their office in the old mill and Angelo explained his position.

He was a dark man of medium height, in his middle thirties, a man on his way up in the organization. He wore an expensive suit and shoes, and he moved as slowly as a snake on a cold day, turning his head to focus his half-open, hooded eyes on each one of the boys as they spoke, then nodding and waiting before he said anything. They were tough, but Angelo was dangerous. He carried a semi auto forty-five beneath his suit coat, and his eyes were flat and cold and bottomless black. Angelo carried a gun to kill people.

"Lemme explain how this is gonna work," Angelo said. "We think you can handle coke, crack, and heroin out here." He shrugged. "How much, I don't know. Could be a lot, could be not so much. Time will tell. We'll make it easy for you. You'll get a big discount for the first six months, then we raise the prices. You don't go outside Wally's Falls. We figure once you're up and running you oughta net maybe a couple hundred grand a year." He stopped and looked at each of them. "So, whattya think?"

Keith, who usually did the talking, spoke first. "We've been doing okay with just pot, Angelo. Nobody bothers us. Maybe we don't make as much, but we don't have to deal with the cops, cause nobody gets too excited about that stuff anymore."

Angelo nodded. "I see your point, there, and I'm gonna grant you it's a good point, but what you gotta understand, in business nothing stands still. You take risks. This here is virgin territory." He stuffed his fingers into the pockets of his suit jacket, the thumbs remaining outside. "Lemme make this clear. You want pot, you gotta sell the other stuff too. You can't get no one else to supply you, without you run the risk of making me angry, and I don't think you boys wanna do that." He laughed, but it was not the sort of laugh that produced merriment in anyone who heard it. "Hey, look at the benefits. We give you free acid for a month. All you can sell. Anything else you need, PCP, speed, you name it, you got it. All you gotta do is build a clientele. Are we clear on this?" They nodded.

"We got a lotta new sales methods. You throw a party somewhere. You supply the beer, which you will get from our distributor, and you put out the invitations, and when everybody's drunk, you start peddling. We'll send bouncers for you, young guys working their way up, but it comes out of the profits, capiche? You have the bouncers handle sales, that way you stay clean. You don't drink, you don't do drugs. You gotta be clear in the head, you gotta have escape exits set up, you gotta be ready for trouble. Am I clear on this? I hope I'm clear on this, because I know you guys smoke up some of the profits, and I'm telling you right now, that's done. You don't get into no trouble. At school you work hard and do what you're told. It's like you turned over a new leaf or something. Am I clear on this?" He looked into each face, nodded, and then went on. "I know you like being tough guys. Hey, like me. I did that, but it went nowhere. The Organization don't like attention. That's why we're keeping you in. It was a smart thing you done, getting rid of them rods. Not many guys woulda thought of that." He pulled his hands from his pockets. "Okay. You got a week to think over how you're gonna get started. Your next shipment of pot will have the other stuff with it. Everything comes packaged and labeled. Everything is the best quality. We even got chemists who check the stuff so nobody gets a reputation for selling bad dope." He looked down at the floor and then back up and his eyes seemed to blaze in the dim light. "The thing you wanna remember — I'm watching. You won't never see me, but I'm watching. You screw with me..." he raised his hand and pointed a finger at Keith's head. "Bang! Very simple. Very clean. No witnesses. No nothing. Just bang and done."

After he had gone, they sat in the dim light of the basement room in the old mill without talking, and then, finally, Richie spoke up. "We don't have much choice."

"So what if we don't," Kyle said as he smoothed his blond curly hair against his head. "I'm in this for the money. The harder we push, the more we make."

"The cops," Keith said. "What about the cops? You think once this stuff gets on the street they aren't gonna know about it? Some jerk'll freak, and then they'll be into it. And who's ass is hanging out? Ours, not Angelo's — right?"

Kyle, the shortest of the three, but by far the nastiest in a fight, just smiled. "The guys that get taken down always have a lot of stuff on them. So we never carry anything. And we never sell to an adult, because the law says they can't use kids undercover anymore."

Keith, tall and thin, settled himself into the low couch, looking like a crane settling onto a tree branch. "I think that's a plan," he said, "but we gotta stick to it. No matter what."

"What's to keep them from telling the cops who they got it from?" Richie asked.

Kyle grinned, raised his hand and pointed it at Richie's head. "Bang!" he said.

"Enough with that bang crap," Keith said. "We got a good deal here. We just gotta be smart for once. We use the bouncers to peddle the drugs, and we show up like anybody else looking for a party. We don't start nothing, we just mingle and look like the rest of the losers. All we do is keep the sales people supplied."

"I say we look for that big freshman kid and teach him a lesson," Kyle said. "He's got it coming."

"Who are you talking about?" Keith asked. "What kid?"

"Foxrucker. The big hero."

"The guy who got the little kids off the school bus?"

"Yeah, that's the guy. He's supposed to be some hot shot football player. Those guys need a lesson." Kyle grinned. "The best part is he's just a freshman, so he can't be very tough."

Keith pointed his finger at Kyle. "Listen, hothead, you do something like that and it's over. You want to get him, we'll take care of that, but not like you think. We spot him and we plant some stuff on him, and then we make sure the cops are looking for him."

Kyle grinned. "I like it," he said. "I like it a lot."

"But it ain't gonna happen right away," Kyle said, "cause the last thing we need is anybody getting busted for dope. That'll send a signal. We gotta build this up so everyone has to be there. The crowd's gotta be big so we don't get spotted."

"Being patient sucks," Kyle said.

"Yeah, but taking him down won't," Richie said.

Keith shook his head. His job was to keep his two hothead friends under control. No fights, not even any shoving matches. And no, absolutely no booze or drugs. That would be the hard part. Richie liked being stoned way too much. "Have either of you guys seen this kid?" They both shook their heads. "I have. He's big and he looks tough. He may be a freshman, but he's no pushover. And another thing. Have you ever seen his old man?"

"No," Kyle said.

"He's built like Arnold Swartzenegger. And he was some kind of big hero in Viet Nam."

"Okay, okay, I got the message," Kyle said.

Chapter Seven

Dark Clouds Rising

Betsy Crenshaw stopped by Damon's locker as he was trying to dig out his algebra book.

"Did you hear about the big party?" she asked.

"No. What party?" Damon dug through his locker, knowing he had put the book and his homework in there before home room.

"It was in one of the old mills. They even had free beer!"

He turned, standing with his right hand draped over the locker door. "Really? Free beer?"

"In kegs."

Damon shrugged. "To go to a party like that you gotta have a driver's license or a friend who drives." He went back to looking for the book, and then suddenly remembered he'd put it in his backpack so he wouldn't have to stop at his locker, because that's where Betsy always caught up to him.

"Or date someone who drives."

He hated it when girls sounded that way. So superior. There was a word for it. Smug. Yeah, smug. Was that right? "I drive, I just don't have a license," he said, knowing it sounded lame but right now he had a lot of things on his mind, not the least of which was the note he'd gotten to see Mr. Waters before lunch. He assumed he'd done something wrong, but for the first time, he knew he hadn't, which left him a little puzzled, but not so puzzled that he didn't know it was bad. It was always bad when you got called to the principal's office. But he was also curious about the party. He looked up at the clock in the hall.

"Not everybody gets to go," she said.

Four minutes to get to class, and normally he would have torn off, but something in Betsy's voice stopped him. "What kind of a party was it?" he asked.

"Beer and dancing. They even had a D.J."

"And nobody had to pay?"

"It was all free."

Damon had a fatal flaw. He never quite believed what people said. Maybe he got it from his father, who never believed anything anyone said. But no matter where it came from, it was there, and it couldn't be ignored.

"Who paid for the beer and the D.J.?" he asked.

"I don't know. But it was really cool." She leaned in close, whispering. "There were even guys selling drugs!"

"Really?"

"And not just weed, either, but coke and crack and even heroin. They just gave away acid. It was wild. People were tripping all over the place."

"Who was selling the drugs? The Rumble Brothers?"

"Some guys I never saw before."

"Let me give you some advice, Bets," he said. "Don't go to another one."

"Why?"

He looked into her soft blue eyes, wondering why some people could never see trouble coming, when he could see it miles and miles away. "What do you think?"

"Oh, the cops."

"Yeah, the cops. Anything that big is gonna get back to them, right? And sooner or later they'll bust everybody in the joint."

"But it's so cool, Damon ... you can't imagine.... And now nobody can say there's nothing to do in Wally's Falls."

He looked up at the clock. "Damn, I'm late!" He took off down the hall at a run, dodging the few other stragglers. He hated to be late for algebra, unlike history or English, which were only good for sleeping through. But math was easy. No guesswork. You did the numbers, you got the answer. Not like English where the teacher could make up the answers.

Mr. Stannard looked at the clock on the back wall as Damon opened the door, walked in, and took his seat. He smiled. "A little lollygagging, Mr. Foxrucker?"

"Yes, sir."

"Most people — I would have marked them late ..." he looked out at the class. "But A students get a little leeway. It might do to remember that."

Damn, Damon thought, my reputation is in the crapper. Cool does not include A grades. And with that out, maybe hanging around with Larry wasn't such a good idea.

It got to be an even worse idea when Mr. Waters explained why he had asked him to come by the office.

"Everyone I've talked to," he said, "told me how you went back into the smoke and made sure everyone got off the bus, and then went back in again to get Larry. In my book that's the stuff of heroes, Damon, and I'd like you and your parents to come to the school board meeting on Thursday so we can present you with an award."

What could he say? "It wasn't really anything, Mr. Waters. Anybody would have done the same."

"But as it happens, plenty of others had the chance and didn't. Only you went back to save those kids."

"But it wasn't even dangerous."

"I don't think you knew that at the time, did you?"

"No, sir."

Mr. Waters smiled. "What strikes me as strange is that you seem sort of reluctant to accept being labeled as a hero."

"No, sir. It's a great honor. I guess, I guess I'm just kind of surprised." He shrugged.

Mr. Water's pale blue eyes suddenly seemed very bright. "A true hero," he said, "sees something that needs to be done and then does it without ever considering the risk." He smiled again. "Like father, like son, I guess."

Damon shook his head. "I don't know about that," he said, "Dad's got a lot of medals."

"Your father is without question the bravest man I know, and in the Marines I knew a lot of very brave men."

"He doesn't talk about it."

"I'm sure he doesn't. Can you think why?"

Damon shrugged.

"Surely you can do better than that."

He knew. "It might be a lot for a kid to live up to."

Mr. Waters laughed. "Exactly!" he said.

Damon nodded, suddenly at a loss for words, a state of affairs which rarely occurred.

"I've already called your parents. I had hoped your father would wear his full dress uniform, but he declined. He sighed. " I'd like this town to know who Harley Foxrucker is, and with all the new people moving in, it seems as if everyone who's always lived here has been forgotten. Most people think he's just a mechanic with a yard full of junk."

"Is that really what they think?" Damon asked.

"It is," Mr. Waters said.

Damon laughed. "Do you know what he really does?"

"I'm not sure that I do."

"He builds monster trucks, stretch limos, and armored passenger cars. He's got twenty guys working for him."

◆ ◆ ◆

It was getting to be a long list, Damon thought, as he waited through the lunch line. A hero who got A's in algebra, didn't think there was anything even the least bit cool about drugs, and hung out with Larry the Rat. But he still played football. As long as he played football he stayed cool.

He sat down with the guys who had worked out together over the weekend. "S'up?"

"You hear about the party?" Roger asked.

"Yeah."

"Pretty wild stuff."

"Crazy stuff," Warren said as he picked up his sandwich. "I got a cousin in the city ... no ... I *had* a cousin in the city. He got into drugs and then gangs and now he's dead."

"Whoa, no way ...." Roger said.

"Got himself shot. He was only twelve."

They all sat quietly, thinking that over, trying to fit it to the way they lived, but it was simply too foreign.

"I'm sorry," Damon said.

Warren shrugged. "My dad kept trying to get them to move out here, but they were afraid."

"Of what?" Joe Santos asked.

Warren grinned. "White people."

"You mean, like, us?" Roger's surprise was clear.

"Haven't you guys ever heard of racism?"

"Sure," Joe said. "Everybody's heard of it, Warren, it's just that out here, I mean.... Do you think we're like that?"

"Some are," Damon said.

"More than you think," Warren said.

"But it's still okay, isn't it?" Roger asked. "I mean like no-body gives you any trouble, do they? Cause if they do ...."

Warren looked around at his friends and it was his turn to be surprised. They were indeed his friends and race didn't matter. If someone picked on a friend you stood up for him. Simple. "You guys look pissed," he said.

"We are," Damon said. "My old man says, everybody gets a chance and the difference between people is what they do with the chance they get."

"And would he stand up for that?" Warren asked.

"You met him," Damon said. "What do you think?"

Warren nodded. "Yeah, he would."

Joe looked at Warren. "What does your dad do?"

"He's an engineer at Barton Machine Tool."

"And my old man runs a grocery store," Joe said, "and Mr. Foxrucker is a mechanic, and Mr. Wilkes owns a dry-cleaning business. Your father is the only one that went to college. No-body in my family ever went to college."

"Mine either, at least on my father's side," Damon said.

"Me too," Roger said.

"But I better," Damon said, "or my mother'll kill me."

"Everybody wants their kids to do better than they did," Warren said. "Human nature."

They turned and looked up as Larry stopped at their table, holding his tray. "You guys mind if I join you?"

"Sit down," Warren said. "I want to hear more about that bike of yours."

"Thanks."

Larry looked particularly short when he sat down, because what little height he had was all in his legs. He looked like a grammar school kid, he sat so low in his chair. "Did you guys hear about the party?"

"That's all anybody's talking about," Roger said.

"There's gonna be another one Saturday night," Larry said.

"I heard two girls talking about it in the line."

Damon shook his head. "It's good I don't have my license."

"Just stay away," Warren said. "Stuff like that always goes bad. Either the cops find out and bust everybody, or somebody overdoses and dies. It's nothing but bad."

"Betsy Crenshaw told me they were giving away acid," Damon said. "That can get out of hand pretty fast."

"I hate stuff like this," Larry said. "Even if you're not part of it, your parents go crazy as soon as they hear about it." He snorted out a laugh. "With my parents that makes it really weird. I mean, it's not like I've got a social life, exactly. With a nose like mine you're at the bottom of the barrel."

Warren looked around at Larry as if he'd never seen him before. "Makes two of us," he said. "Not many black girls here."

"Racism?" Damon asked.

"When it comes to dating someone's daughter, race is all that counts."

"Warren," Joe said, "I got cousins darker than you."

"But they aren't black."

"Well neither are you, at least totally," Larry said. "Nobody is pure-bred. I'm English, Irish, and German."

"My grandmother's French," Warren said. "And I got another grandmother who was Cajun."

"That's what I mean," Larry said. "Why should you be called black? It's only a part of what you are."

"But what about my slave name ... Wilson?"

"It's probably not a slave name," Larry said. "I read that most slaves weren't allowed to have surnames, but they picked names and used them in secret, and then after the Civil War they had full names. But they didn't pick the names of their owners. They picked names they liked, or maybe from somebody they admired. That slave name stuff is bunk."

"Is there anything you don't know something about?" Warren asked.

"Football. And even after this weekend I still don't know much about football. But I'm gonna learn, 'cause you're looking at your new manager. I signed up this morning."

"Now that's cool," Warren said.

Damon grinned. "Why didn't I think of that? I knew we needed a manager, but I just never thought of it."

"Probably because a guy with a legendary schnozz who blows up school buses didn't come to mind as a manager."

They all laughed and Larry could feel himself move one step closer to acceptance. And if these guys did finally accept him, his nose would grow smaller in the eyes of the girls, or at least he hoped it would. "I think we all should spread the word to stay away from those parties. I got a premonition. Something very bad is gonna happen there."

"Like what?" Warren asked.

Larry shrugged. "All I know is that those guys are bad. Twice they tried to knock me off my bike with a car."

"What guys?" Roger asked.

"The Rumbles? Is that what you call them?"

"The Rumble Brothers," Warren said. "You think they're behind this?"

"Different cars, same guys," Larry said. "I can't find anyone who saw them there, but their cars were parked out back."

Damon sat back in his chair and folded his arms across his chest. "Maybe they need a lesson."

"Not from me," Warren said. "My old man would have my ass in traction for a month. He's got a rule about fighting, and he hates gangs of any kind."

"But we're not a gang," Joe said.

"We would be if we got together and went after them." Damon shook his head. "Warren's right. Just play football and get good grades. Then you've got some choices."

Chapter Eight

Grinding on the Gridiron

Practice. It was supposed to make you perfect, but here they were on Friday, after another week of butting heads like a bunch of energized goats, and they were no further along. Which meant they'd get their butts kicked against Wilberfield tomorrow.

It's also hard to see, Damon thought, how Bunker thinks I'm gonna know what to do if anything happens to Ricky, because I never got to practice. All I do is sit on the bench, read the play book, and watch Ricky making handoffs. No passes. Not even any pitchouts. He just doesn't like the ball in the air.

Damon closed the play book, set it on the bench, and picked up a football, wrapping his right hand around it, flexing his fingers against the pebbled leather surface. Last year Wilberfield had finished second in the state and they had most of that team back. They've got two good runners and a good quarterback. Our only hope is to play solid defense, and at least we're getting better there. The linebackers are big and fast and mean and Aaron Blesser is a wizard at free safety. But Wilberfield's got a powerful offense, and given time that'll wear any defense down, especially when your offense goes three downs and punts, because that leaves the defense on the field most of the time.

He stood up, stretched, thinking about how Ricky didn't hide the ball on his handoffs. Deception was the only way you could make a ground game work ... that and the pass. If you didn't throw, the other team pulled the secondary up, and they nailed any back that got past the line.

He was standing on the sidelines watching Larry hovering nearby with the air horn, when Coach turned toward him. "Foxrucker! Get out here!"

Damon grabbed his helmet and ran out onto the field.

"Okay, Foxrucker. I want you to run some simple plays."

"Yes sir."

"First try a thirty-two slant."

Damon nodded, snapped the strap on his helmet, and stepped into the huddle. "Okay, thirty-two slant on one." They broke and lined up and he settled in behind the center.

"Set! Fifty-six, thirty-five, Hut One!"

The ball slammed back into his hands and he turned away immediately, concealing the handoff with his body, and then carrying the fake to the right, keeping his hands and arms in as if he were carrying the ball, and the defense went for it. He faked and slid through the line, then faked again before the defense turned toward Harry Contaglio, who had followed the guard off tackle, slanting between the linebackers. He made fifteen yards before they pulled him down from behind. It was the first time all day that a play had gone for more than three yards.

"Now that's football!" Coach shouted. "That's the best BLAAAT-ing play we've run today!"

Damon walked over to him, waiting for the next call.

"Nice move, Foxrucker. Nice move," he said. "Okay, this time run the fifty-three option right."

He took the snap and ran down the line to his right as Contaglio ran parallel to him, looking for the pitch, but Damon could see the outside linebacker lining up on Contaglio, and he faked the pitch, pivoted on his left foot, and shot back through a hole in the line, and while he wasn't fast, he was very tricky. Ten yards, fifteen yards, twenty yards, and he was in the open, headed for the end zone, with Aaron Blesser coming fast ... very fast, and worse, he had the angle. All Damon could do was wait until Aaron left his feet. And then he stiff-armed him, using Aaron's weight to push off, spin, and break clear.

The guys on offense were jumping and hollering as if they'd just won the state championship, pounding him on his shoulder pads as he trotted back.

Bunker looked like he'd seen a ghost, he stood with his arms at his sides, his mouth open, simply staring at Damon as if he could not believe what he'd just seen. Only slowly did it begin to dawn on him whose son he was watching.

"All right, Foxrucker. Now that's football!" He leaned in close, whispering, "try the same play again."

Damon stepped into the huddle. "Now listen up. If I get to the line and call out the word post, just block the way you usually would." He caught Warren's grin.

They broke the huddle and as he approached the line he checked the defense. They were lined up to stop the option. The secondary was pulled in close and the outside linebacker was keyed on Harry. "Post! Twenty-six, twenty-seven, hut one, hut two!" The ball came back harder, and he started down the line, holding the ball by his right leg, and then suddenly he rolled back deeper, and when Warren cleared the secondary, he turned and let it fly, a long spiral, that hit Warren's hands perfectly, and Warren cut in his afterburners and he was gone.

"What the BLAAAT was that! A BLAAAT-ing pass? Who said you could BLAAAT-ing pass?"

Damon shrugged. "I just thought they wouldn't be looking for it, Coach, and besides, they had Harry covered."

"I want you to understand something, Foxrucker! The

BLAAAT-ing forward pass is a gimmick! It ruined football! It's like cheating on an exam! You're benched!"

Damon shrugged and walked away as Ricky trotted past him. "Nice going, Foxrucker. You just ended your season."

Damon pulled off his helmet and dropped it on the ground next to the bench. Why couldn't he have waited till he got into a game? Then when Bunker benched him, the people in the stands would gotten on his case. It was dumb. But it was the kind of stuff he'd always done. Either he spouted off or he did something like this. Dumb. No. Not dumb. Just impatient. But how could you be patient and play football?

He didn't know anyone was close by until he saw a pair of Nikes. He looked up.

"That wasn't the smartest thing I've ever seen," Coach Zander said.

Damon shrugged.

They both looked out at the field as Larry sounded the air horn again and then again. Damon laughed.

But Mr. Zander didn't. "You need to understand something, Foxrucker. George Bunker was a great player in his day. He set all kinds of records for Ohio State. He played four years with the Bears. He knows the game. I'll admit he's got a quirk about passing, but that doesn't give you the right to laugh at him."

"I was laughing at Larry. His timing's off with the horn."

Zander ignored him. "That stunt you just pulled ruined your chances of ever getting into a game. Do you know that?"

"I'll probably quit then," Damon said.

"I think you might as well."

"I think some guys will go with me."

"You certainly have a high opinion of yourself."

"No. I have a low opinion of Bunker."

"Big mouth too."

"Yup."

"What makes you think anyone else will quit?"

"Why do people play football?" Damon asked.

"What kind of a question is that?"

"A question. Do you know the answer?"

"Of course I know the answer."

"I thought you would. Coaches know everything."

"Are you trying to make me angry? Is that it?"

Damon shrugged. "If you know the answer, then you know they'll quit."

He sighed. "All right, Foxrucker, what's the answer."

"To win."

"That isn't it at all. That has nothing to do with football. You play because you love the game. Competition in sports is out. It's an eighties thing."

"Is that why owners fire coaches who don't win?"

"I can't account for all those idiots who won't go to a game unless their team wins, but that doesn't matter. That's a business. This is education."

Damon shrugged.

"I suppose you think I'm wrong, don't you?"

It was a crucial point. If he kept his mouth shut, it would pass, but Zander was too big a target. "Maybe if you'd played football, you wouldn't think like a mother," Damon said.

"Okay, that's it! I've had enough of your insolence! You shower up and report to the principal's office!"

◆　◆　◆

"Uh-oh." Mr. Waters looked up from his desk at Damon, standing with his cleats under his arm, still in his practice uniform, pain showing clearly in his eyes. "Looks like you got into it again, huh?"

"Yes, sir."

"What happened this time?"

"Bunker won't let me play because I'm too good."

Mr. Waters laughed. "I like it. It's fresh, original. I never heard it before." He sat back and folded his hands behind his head as Mr. Zander came stomping into the office, his face red with fury.

Mr. Waters held up his hand, palm forward. "Calm down Pete. You look like you're about to blow a zerk."

Damon grinned. It was definitely cool that the principal knew the name for a grease fitting.

Zander whirled toward Damon. "I told you to shower up! Can you tell me why you refuse to follow orders?"

Damon shrugged. Now it was time to keep quiet.

"Harmon, I want him placed on immediate suspension!"

"First," Mr. Waters said, "I think it might be nice if someone would tell me what happened."

"Insubordination! Flagrant insubordination!"

"What did he do?"

"That's unimportant! It was how he did it!"

"Pete, I'd appreciate it if you wouldn't tell me how to do my job, it's kind of irritating. Just tell me what happened."

"He threw a pass, and Coach Bunker benched him. Then he said he might quit and others would also quit."

Harmon nodded. "He's certainly free to do that." He turned to Damon. "Why would you quit?"

"Coach won't play me now, so what's the point?"

Again Mr. Waters nodded. "Because you threw a pass."

"Yes, sir."

"And if you don't pass, you won't win, right?"

"Yes, sir."

"He doesn't get it, Harmon, he just doesn't get it! I tried to explain to him that high school football is not about winning. Winning is an outmoded concept, a dinosaur from the past."

Mr. Waters sighed. "I don't think we want to get into that just now, Pete," he said.

Zander ignored him. "Times have changed, Harmon. The

world is different. We do things differently now."

"We should talk about this another time," Mr. Waters said.

"You always want to put things off. You never want to talk about current trends in education."

Harmon stood up, towering over them, his shoulders squared, and still Zander didn't get the message.

"I'm warning you, Harmon, something has got to be done about this!"

"More warm and fuzzy crap," Mr. Waters said. "Let me explain, Pete, that warm and fuzzy does not happen on the gridiron. Football happens on the gridiron and football is competitive or its not worth playing. I know some of the faculty don't like competition because people get left behind. Let me make this clear. People who don't compete get left behind."

"Well, we'll just see about that."

"Now that, I think, was a threat. You know, I've bent over backward for the faculty, but I guess I'm getting tired of it. So I'm relieving you of your duties as an assistant football coach."

"On what basis?"

"Threatening an administrator, which, by the way is enough for me to put you on leave without pay until the hearing."

"You'll have to prove that."

Mr. Waters grinned. "I think I have a witness here."

"A boy? A mere boy? Who would ever believe a boy?"

"Me," Mr. Waters said.

"I'll file a grievance, you know."

"Of course you will. And I'll ask that the hearing be public, and I'll make sure the newspapers are there, and then I won't have to fire you, because you'll be laughed out of town." He sat down. "Now if you would excuse us, I'd like to talk to Damon before he makes a mistake he'll regret."

"You can't dismiss me like that! I'm tenured. I have rights!"

"I'm asking you to leave," Mr. Waters said.

Mr. Zander crumpled. "Now you're pressuring me. I'll have

to see my doctor. I may have to take a leave of absence for stress."

"Pete, just leave will you?"

'I don't have to take this, you know."

"Just go."

Zander turned and left the office.

Mr. Waters shook his head and sat quietly for several minutes and then he looked up at Damon. "You shouldn't have been here for that."

Damon nodded.

"Coach Bunker was a fullback at Ohio State when they went out to play in the Rose Bowl. They were undefeated. Everybody thought they were unstoppable. And then they ran into a quarterback from Southern Cal who handed them the worst defeat in Ohio State's history and Coach Bunker never got over it. He went into the pros and all they used him for was a blocker to protect the quarterback." He shook his head. "He's not a bad guy, Damon. In fact he's a good guy. I'll talk to him, but I can't guarantee he'll change." He grinned. "I saw your practices in the park, by the way. You've got a heck of a talent, young man."

He shifted gears again. "Now, what's going on in English? You scored in the ninty-fifth percentile on the entry exam but you're only doing C work. How do you explain that?"

Damon shrugged. "Mrs. Haroldson. I wrote an essay about football, and she downgraded me for writing about sports."

Mr. Waters sighed and shook his head slowly. "I'll talk to her," he said. "Okay, now here's the way it's going to shake out. As long as you stay on the team, you have a chance to play. What you did this afternoon will be all over school by tomorrow. Every parent of every player is going to hear about it. And then if we don't win, they're going to demand to know why you didn't play. Get the picture?"

Damon grinned.

"And thanks for taking off your cleats," Mr. Waters said.

Chapter Nine

The Ball Begins to Bounce

Wilberfield won the coin toss, elected to receive the kickoff, scored in six plays, kicked the extra point, and led by seven. You wouldn't have thought Wally's Falls had any players on the field.

Then came the Wilberfield defense. Monsters. Even the secondary guys were at least six feet tall. Damon just shook his head. The only hope was to find a weakness in the defense somewhere, but it would have to be a bigger weakness than the one he'd found in the offense.

He stood up and walked over to Tim Black the defensive captain. "Hey, Tim," he said. "They look tough, huh?"

Tim just grunted. He was a senior and he didn't talk to freshmen, especially he didn't talk to freshmen who were cocky and in trouble with the coach.

"Look, I know I'm only a freshman, but I saw something that might help you guys."

"Yeah ... right ...."

"No. Seriously."

"Just 'cause your father was a big star, don't think you know anything about football."

Damon sighed, and looked down at his feet. "You know, some guys might get pissed at a remark like that, but I got one thing on my mind here. I don't like losing."

Maybe it was something in his voice, maybe in the way he looked, or in the intensity of his gaze, but suddenly Tim nodded. "Okay, tell me."

"When the right guard gets ready to pull on a running play, he sets his feet wider than usual. When it's a pass play, the wideout bends over more. Not much, but it's something to work on. I mean, at least you'll know when to put a hit on him."

"You need to play more football, kid. Nobody has time to look for that stuff."

"Quarterbacks do, and there's not much difference between a quarterback and a middle linebacker."

Tim looked at him closely for a second or so and then shook his head again. Freshmen, And then he remembered practice and the way this kid could fake and run ... and there was no denying he could pass. And on the pass play he'd checked off at the line of scrimmage when he saw how the defense was set up. In three years, Ricky hadn't learned how to do that. And another thing. He wasn't afraid to take a hit or throw a block.

The ref blew his whistle and Damon watched Wilberfield's defense set up. They knew what play was coming because bunker never changed anything. It came, and so did the defense, the middle linebacker shooting through and nailing Ricky in the middle of the handoff. You could hear the hit for half-a-mile as Ricky went one way, the ball went the other, and Wilberfield recovered the fumble on the Wally's Falls' fifteen. It took Wilberfield one play, a slant pass to the tight end. Fourteen zip.

Damon looked around at Ricky, standing next to Bunker, and shook his head. One more hit like that and he was done for the day. You can't get your bell rung like that too many times before your legs go wobbly and your vision clouds.

He looked up as Warren set himself at his ten yard line to take the kickoff. They even had a monster kicker and he sent it into the end zone. Bunker Rule: down any kickoff you take in the end zone and start at the twenty. Bunker Rule broken. Warren took the ball, ran right at the wedge his players were forming in the middle of the field, then ten yards away he slipped to the side, faked the jock off the player coming at him, leaped over another guy on the ground, and cut in his jets. He was fast, lightning-bolt fast, and a second later he had only the kicker to beat, and it was no contest.

Fourteen-seven and the Wally's Falls' fans were going wild. Damon turned and looked at the crowd, and that's when he saw Jenny Simmons with the cheerleading squad. She was so pretty it made his knees weak just to look at her. And she was looking at him. She smiled, raised her hand only as high as her shoulder, and waved. He waved back, feeling a solid blush creep out from under his uniform and up to his face. Now he wanted to get into the game even more. His parents were there, and Uncle Paul had made the drive up from mid-state, and even his grandparents had come to the game ... just to watch him ride the bench.

He turned at the whistle and watched the kickoff sail into the hands of Wilberfield's deep back. He ran right up into the wedge, but the guy who was supposed to have taken out Melvin Upshaw got flattened, and Melvin crunched the runner, hitting him mid-thigh, and driving him backward. There was nothing like scoring a touchdown to get you excited, Damon thought.

But the Wilberfield offense was pissed. Damon watched the quarterback's feet. On a pass play he kept his left foot back. On a running play his feet were almost even. But this time it was not so easy because Tim had, after all, passed on what he'd seen, and the secondary knew when they could drop coverage on the wide receiver. They stuffed the first running play by bringing a back up into the hole. Then they called the wide receiver's number and he tipped them off by bending over more, and they doubled the coverage and knocked the ball away.

But Wilberfield had a big bag of tricks, and on the next play they ran a screen pass to the tailback, and it suckered the whole line and the linebackers as they rushed the quarterback. He waited until they were committed, and then tossed a short pass to his tailback, who had three blockers in front of him. He went the length of the field.

Twenty-one to seven. This time they kicked the ball away from Warren, keeping it low so it scooted through the end zone before he could get to it. He grinned. Warren was still playing, which meant that you could break a Bunker rule and still play. The offense started at the twenty and ended, three plays later, on the five. Ricky was very slow getting to his feet, and even when he got up he staggered off the field. Not much longer, Damon thought. Not much longer and he has to put me in.

After the punt, the defense did an even better job, and for the first time Wilberfield had to punt.

Tim was smiling at him as he came off the field. "Hey, Foxrucker," he said, "I gotta hand it to you, man. You were dead nuts on. Their coach must be going crazy trying to figure out how we saw those plays coming." He stepped in close. "Now all we gotta do is find a way to get you into the game. I even think we could beat these guys."

Damon nodded. "I picked up something else. The quarterback cheats with his left foot on a pass play."

"Did I understand right? Your dad is really Harley Foxrucker?"

"Yeah."

"My dad says you got a lot to live up to."

Damon grinned. "Better that the other way, huh?"

"Big-time pressure."

"All I want to do is get into the game."

"And put the ball in the air."

"Yup."

"And then sit on the bench."

He shrugged. The Offense was going nowhere. The first play got stuffed at the line for no gain. The second play was a pitch out, and it lost four yards which left them with a third down and fourteen yards to go to get a first down. Worse, Ricky was down, flat on his back, and he was not getting up.

Bunker ran out onto the field and squatted down next to his quarterback. "Ricky, Ricky, can you hear me?"

Ricky nodded.

"How many fingers am I holding up?" He held up two.

"Three?" Ricky said.

Bunker seemed to sag. "Can you get up?"

"I'm pretty dizzy, coach."

Bunker stood up and waved to the guys at the ambulance. They came running out and knelt next to Ricky, asking him questions, checking him over. Finally one of them looked up. "It looks like a mild concussion," Coach. "I think a doctor should take a look at him just to be safe."

Bunker stood watching them bring the ambulance out onto the field, stabilize Ricky's neck, load him in, and drive off.

"Foxrucker!"

Damon pulled on his helmet and trotted out onto the field. Great athletes have a bearing, a way of standing, walking, and trotting. They look explosive, as if they are nothing more than energy about to be released. They are tense and loose at the same time, and that's what Harley Foxrucker saw as his son trotted onto the field. Damon was in the right place at the right time and he knew it.

For the first time Coach Bunker saw it to, but what he also saw was a tall California kid with an arm that could throw football bullets through a January afternoon in Pasadena; a kid who had destroyed one of the best teams ever assembled at Ohio State. He swallowed hard, looking down at the grass so bright and green, as he thought about what he had seen in the park a week ago, and about his conversation with Harmon. He was tired of losing football games. "You know how I feel, Foxrucker."

"Yes, Sir."

"One question. Why doesn't the offense work?"

Damon looked down at his coach, wondering whether this was some sort of trap. But whether it was or not, he only had one way to answer. "Ricky doesn't know how to hide the ball and ... they always know it's going to be a run."

Coach Bunker nodded. "Yeah, that about sums it up."

"But the pass only works if the ground game keeps them honest. Coach, we can run against these guys. They're slow off the snap. But right now I gotta throw a pass to get the first down, and I need to have Warren and Roger in the game."

"What are you going to throw?"

"Post pattern. They're playing man coverage in the backfield, and the guy who'll draw Warren can't cover him."

Bunker nodded. He was Harley's boy all right.

The ref walked over to them. "Coach, you ready to play?"

"Ready," he said. Then he slapped Damon on the butt. "You do what you have to, kid," he said. "Maybe I'm not too old to learn after all." He turned to the bench. "Wilson, take Sanders' place. Wilkes in for Haroldson."

Warren and Roger shot off the bench and ran for the huddle, getting there as Damon crouched down to call the play. "Okay," he said, "listen up. Block for a 96 pass. Snap on four. But be alert I'm gonna stagger the count. When I get to three, I'll stop and count to four. When I call hut we go."

They broke and moved up to the line. "Ready! Set! One ... two ... three ...." The Wilberfield nose guard anticipated the count and crashed offside. The ref blew his whistle and called the penalty. Five yards. That left them only nine for the first down, but more importantly it confused the defense, because it denied them the advantage of following an even count.

Damon called the same play and this time the defense stayed honest, but that gave the offensive line an advantage, allowing them to come up out of their stances and into their blocks, and that meant they could control the blocks and protect the passer.

Damon dropped back three steps and fired a rifle of a pass to Warren on the fly through the middle of the secondary. It caught Wilberfield absolutely flatfooted. In the blink of an eye Warren was through and on his way to his second touchdown. Twenty-one to fourteen.

In the stands, as they sat back down, Grace turned to her husband. "Harley, did he do a good job? Did he do it right?"

Harley nodded and grinned as he folded his arms over his chest. "You have no idea how right."

Paul leaned over. "Damn, Harley, that was one hell of a pass! He put that ball in his receiver's hands right on stride. I mean, the kid looked up, and the ball was there, and all he had to do was put his hands on it."

Grace smiled. "Doing it that way, that's a good thing, right?"

"Grace," Harley said. "Over the next eight years you're gonna watch a lot of games."

"How do you know that?"

"Because he's doing what he was born to do."

The whole tenor and flavor of the game had changed. The Wilberfield players had come onto the field, certain of winning, and now they faced a team that believed it could win. The defense was inspired, and Wilberfield went three plays and punted, and Wally's Falls wound up with the ball on their own forty in fine position to start another drive.

Wilberfield expected the pass, but instead got a handoff that went for ten yards and a first down, and then a quarterback option that went for fifteen. Their coach called a time out and turned to his assistants. "Okay," he said, "how come I don't know about this kid? I mean, I'm looking at maybe the best young quarterback I ever saw, and nobody knows anything about him? I don't even know his name."

One of the assistants looked down the list of players. "Damon Foxrucker," he said. "Funny name."

The coach looked as if he had swallowed a frog. "Not so damn funny," he said. "I played against his father and his uncles. They killed us. Now I get to watch another Foxrucker for four years. Sometimes there isn't any justice."

And on that Saturday in September there was no justice for Wilberfield. On the next play they double covered Warren and that left Roger Wilkes wide open on the left side. Damon threw it cross-field, on the run, and Roger just trotted into the end zone. Twenty-one to twenty-one.

After that, the running game exploded. Damon used the pass when he needed it, but he kept the ball on the ground and ate up the clock. Penalties helped, and the exasperated Wilberfield players committed one foul after another. The final score was forty-two to twenty-one. Wally's Falls had won their first game in two years, and the team carried Damon off the field.

Afterward, before he showered, Damon sat in Coach Bunker's office.

"You know, Damon, you really surprised me out there this afternoon. You know the play book cold. I had this idea that all you wanted to do was throw the ball, but you used my plays and you made them work."

"My dad always says that for a play to work everyone has to do their job. Once our guys got pumped they did that. But you still have to have good plays."

"But do you know why it worked?"

"They found out that they could do it."

"No. They found a leader. We've got a quarterback who led his team."

"Coach, Mr. Waters told me about the Rose Bowl."

"He did?"

"Yes, sir."

"So you understand then."

"Yes, sir."

"The real reason they beat us that day was the way he ran the game. He even called his own plays on the field. I'd never seen anything like it. I can understand that in a guy who's a senior in college. But here you are, a freshman in high school, and you called your own plays, and you changed plays at the line of scrimmage too." He shook his head. "I think I am finally going to enjoy a football season," he said. "It's been a long time." He grinned. "I may not even need the air horn anymore."

Damon stood up. "Coach, I know that wasn't easy today."

Coach Bunker stood up. "You're right. But the reason it wasn't is because I was being a blockhead. I know this game. I know probably as much as anyone can know about this game, and I ignored what I learned in Pasadena." He grinned. "The best part is that from here on we just play football ... the way it was meant to be played." He clapped Damon on the arm. "Just keep your grades up and your nose clean. Right?"

"Yes, sir."

"You don't and I'll be talking to your father, and unless he's changed over the years, that's one guy I wouldn't care to answer to."

"It won't be a problem, Coach." He looked down at his feet and then back up. "How's Ricky?"

"He's fine. Slight concussion. But he's out for several weeks until his doctor clears him."

"I'm glad he wasn't hurt badly."

"It's part of the game," Coach said.

"He's a good guy."

Coach Bunker nodded. "Feeling sorry?"

"Nope." He shrugged. "If he'll listen, I can show him how to hide the ball better, and then the plays will work. I can even help him with his passing. You always need a backup."

Chapter Ten

Forever Changed

John Falworth picked up Barbara Johnson and Betsy Crenshaw at Barbara's house at nine o'clock. Had it been any other way, Betsy would not have gone because her parents did not allow her, at fourteen, to go out on dates, and especially they did not allow her to ride around in cars with boys. Barbara's parents could have cared less.

It was a standard arrangement. Stay overnight at a friend's, and as long as her parents didn't say anything, you could go anywhere. Betsy knew that if she got caught, she'd be grounded for the rest of her life, but it just didn't matter. You had to have a life. You had to be free. And after all, she was fourteen. It wasn't like she was still a little kid. Even so, as she climbed into the car, she thought about her little sisters and her mother and father, and the kind of things that could happen to her. Just as quickly, she dismissed those thoughts. What could possibly happen? They'd have a few beers, dance, and be home by midnight just like last time. It was so cool.

With the CD player roaring outrageous tunes, they drove

to the old Perkins Mill. The four-story building backed up to the abandoned railroad line and a cemetery. The front of the building faced West Street and then ran down the next side street to the loading dock entrance. Around back they could park out of sight from any vantage point.

The party was held in the cellar. The only windows were on the back wall, and they had been carefully covered with heavy black cloth. The walls were thick, a foot of solid stone, and very little sound escaped, though the Rumble Brothers were careful to keep the decibel level down, on the off chance that some one walking past might hear.

Inside it was paradise: no adults, free beer, and music. And everywhere they went the talk was all about Damon. Anyone who had been to the game could talk about nothing else, and at first she found it very exciting, and then a little depressing. Her chances of going out with him now were probably about zero.

"It's weird," she said to John, "you'd think he was like some kind of god to hear them talk."

"Just another dumb football player," John said. "Guys like that piss me off. Hell, anybody can do something like that."

Betsy looked down at her shoes. They were great shoes, stylish, and it was the first pair she'd owned that were cool. It had been a two-week fight to talk her mother into letting her get them. "I don't know," she said, "he really was pretty amazing."

"One game. That was just one game."

"But he's only a freshman, John."

"Hey, all I can say is, football is not cool, okay. Just a bunch of muscleheads. But this? This is cool!"

"I think you're jealous," she said.

He snorted out a laugh and polished off the beer in his large paper cup. "Hey, guys like that go nowhere. I mean, look around. You see him here? If he's so cool, why isn't he here?"

And then with a clarity of vision she had seldom experienced before, Betsy thought, no, it's guys like you who are going nowhere, and that thought changed everything. Suddenly she wanted to be away from all this, because now she was frightened by what she saw. These kids were totally out of control. Right in front of her one girl took off her shirt and began dancing. Why would anyone do such a thing? Just because there was nobody there to stop her? What was going on in her mind? Anything? And then she remembered Damon's warning, and that frightened her even more. "John, how long are we staying?"

"The party's just starting. I'm not leaving 'til at least midnight." He rested his hand on her shoulder. "Com'on, Betsy, relax, have a good time. That's what this is all about."

Betsy tried another sip of beer, but now it tasted oddly bitter, where minutes before it had seemed sweet and wild. She set the cup down and walked away, feeling terribly alone. None of her friends from school were here, except Barbara. Most of the kids were juniors and seniors. As she stood there looking around, a guy, a much older guy, came up behind her. "Hey," he said, "I got some really heavy stuff here. Mary Jane. Right from South of the Border. You're looking at thirty-five percent, babe. One puff and your troubles are gone, you dig?"

"No thanks," she said. He was at least six inches taller, and she had never seen him before, and she didn't like him. He was pushy and hard, and his long black hair was tied in a pony tail, and she definitely didn't like guys with pony tails.

"Why? Because parents are so down on drugs? What the hell do parents know about anything? This stuff is cool. One hit and you're flying." He grinned. "Hey, babe, the price is right." He let his gaze wander over her, and she felt as if he could see right through her clothes. She felt cheap.

"I don't do drugs," she said, but even as she heard herself, she knew she hadn't been forceful enough.

"Sure you do, babe. Hey, everybody does drugs. And anyway, I'm not talking crack or coke, I'm talking weed. This stuff can't hurt you. All it does is make you feel cool."

She shook her head. "I need some air," she said.

He shrugged. "Hey, whatever turns you on, babe."

Betsy headed for the door, but the bouncer stopped her.

"Nobody goes out unless they go for good," he said. "And you can't hang around outside, either. Too easy to spot. Sorry."

"Okay," she said.

She walked to the farthest end of the cellar, climbed halfway up a set of stairs, and sat down. Here, at least, she was away from the smoke, but it was going to be a long, long wait.

She passed the time by trying to figure out how many kids were there, but they were too closely packed and constantly moving. She saw a kid roll up his sleeve, slip a needle into his arm and push down on the plunger. How could anyone do something like that? What could they possibly think of themselves? Or was it the drugs? Once they got stoned, they just didn't care.

From her vantage point on the stairs, she could see out over the heads of the people in the huge room. And then she noticed that as time passed, they were less and less excited. There were kids getting sick, kids lying on the floor, passed out. She saw the guy who had tried to sell her marijuana, working his way through the crowd, and now she saw six others doing the same thing, and suddenly she understood. It was a set up to sell drugs. If she had been frightened before, now she was terrified. People like this carried guns and they shot people for no reason at all.

She pulled herself into a small bundle, hoping to hide in the open on the stairs. She slid down four stairs and sat in the dark, leaning against the cold stone of the wall. As long as nobody approached her, she'd be okay. She began to think about how she had ignored the rules her parents had made. It just seemed as if they were always trying to control her for no reason that she could see. But now, she did see. And what she saw was what she had known in some dark part of her mind, was true, but which she had been unwilling to recognize. They were trying to protect her by keeping her from getting into situations she couldn't handle. Like this. And what made that very clear was that the kids here were mostly older, and they were no better at taking care of themselves than a two-year-old. Okay, she said to herself, what you have to do now is get home safely.

A sudden shout and the sound of a fist hitting someone's face got her attention, and she watched two boys square off and began throwing punches. One of them was already bleeding from the nose, and the other boy, bigger and older, was circling him, looking for the chance to hit him again. Nobody tried to break it up. Instead they stood in a circle, laughing and taunting the little guy. The big kid was fast and vicious, and he moved in and hit the smaller kid again and knocked him down, and then when the kid tried to get up, he kicked him in the side, and suddenly a girl screamed at him to stop. When she grabbed his arm, he hit her in the face, and sent her flying into the crowd.

Out of nowhere the guys selling drugs moved in, two of the bigger guys grabbing the guy who was standing. He struggled, trying to twist away from them, shouting, calling them all sorts of names, and then one of the guys hit him in the stomach and the fight just went out of him. Two other guys jerked the little guy to his feet and half-carried him to the door, opened it, and threw him out into the night. The other guy had disappeared, and Betsy wondered what had happened to him, whether he had just melted into the crowd, or whether they had taken him somewhere. But whatever came of it, now everything had changed. The fight had cast a pall across the room, and though the music still played, people just stood around, looking at the floor, uneasy in the way they glanced from side to side. Slowly a few of them began to drift toward the door.

Betsy stood up, looking for Barbara and John. When she spotted them, she began working her way through the crowd. It was like walking through a thick forest, and she had to keep stopping and jumping up to make sure she was headed in the right direction.

"Wow," John said, "did you see that? I thought he was gonna kill that guy!"

"I think we ought to get out of here," Betsy said.

"Why? This is just too cool to end," John said.

Betsy bit her lip, trying to summon the courage to argue. She no longer cared whether she looked like a nerd. "John," she said, "I have to get home!"

Barbara looked at her closely, and then reached out and took John's arm. "Why don't we go home," she said.

John grinned around at her, understanding what she was saying. "Yeah, cool," he said.

Not until they got outside did she realize how drunk John was. He could hardly walk in a straight line, and now another of her parent's warnings rang all too clear. Never get into a car with a drunk driver. But what choice did she have? Neither she nor Barbara could drive, and it was at least a five-mile walk to her house and farther to Barbara's.

"John, are you okay?" she asked.

"Cool, everything's cool."

"I think you're pretty drunk," she said.

"Hey! You saying I shouldn't drive? Get in the car, bitch!"

"What if...."

Barbara grabbed her arm. "Just get in the car before he gets really pissed. Unless you wanna walk."

She climbed into the back seat and closed the door, holding her arms folded across her chest, her head down. Maybe he'd be okay. If he just didn't drive too fast, it would be okay. She was sure of it. No. She was not sure of it. She was scared and she was shaking, and she could feel the tears start to slide down her cheeks. God, how she wanted to be home and safe.

Chapter Eleven

The Night Rider

Sometimes all he could do was get on his bike and go, picking a long route, and then pushing himself to ride at top speed. At night, he wore special riding gear with stripes so bright they seemed to explode when car lights hit him. As his muscles warmed he rode faster and faster over the gentle roll and pitch of the countryside.

It was the only way he knew to clear away anger and frustration and regain control of his emotions. Often enough, he thought, allowing for a certain amount of irony, those emotions seemed to peak on Saturday nights when he was sitting at home feeling sorry for himself. This had been a particularly nasty night, in part because of Damon's astonishing success in the afternoon.

Nothing new. Just the old jealousy like a fire in his brain. But now it was worse. Now he felt guilty about being jealous because he was jealous of a friend. And yet, how could he not be jealous? Damon could get any girl he wanted now. He was a star. A hero. He could have it all. And the truth of the matter was that he wanted the same things. He wanted to be a star and a hero, and that was never going to happen to a guy who spent his life in a chem lab. Nothing helped except riding, working harder and harder, never letting up, so that when he reached home he was ready for a shower and bed. Then in the morning he'd be okay again ... maybe, just maybe, because now the problem was how to get a date for the prom. How many girls would he have to call, a hundred? He didn't know five!

Maybe he could cold-call them the way his father had to do in sales sometimes. "Hi, this is Larry the Rat, and I wondered if you might be in need of a date for the prom?" Need? Nobody *needed* a date for the prom. People didn't need dates for proms. But there must be lots of girls who didn't have dates for the prom. After all, not all girls were beauty queens, any more than all guys were the Mr. Studly Hero type like Damon. There he was, running down Damon again. How dumb was that? The only guy from the other side who had laughed with him instead of at him. "Calm down, Mr. Rat," he told himself aloud. "Go back to thinking about the girls."

The next step was to gather information. Maybe the other guys could help, especially Roger, because he'd had more dates than Casanova.

He felt the anger ease but he was taking no chances. He wanted the gauge back to zero by the time he got home, so he turned and headed out into the country, taking the longest of his routes. Thirty miles. If that didn't calm him down nothing would. And now in the chilly fall air, he congratulated himself for having remembered his jacket. Without it, sweating in the cold air, his body temperature would have dropped too rapidly, and he'd have wound up with a cold.

◆　◆　◆

"Where are we going?" Betsy asked from the back seat.
"Haven't you ever been parking before?" Barbara asked.

"No."

"You can watch, we don't care."

"Barbara, I just want to go home, okay?"

"Sure. It'll just be a while longer."

She looked out the window, aware now that they were going very fast. "John, would you please slow down?"

"Hey, no problem," he said, and then he increased the speed and laughed. "This is a true joy ride."

Betsy pulled her seat belt over her shoulder, making sure the latch was secure. Her hands were shaking, and everything outside looked as if someone had run a finger through a painting that hadn't dried. She glanced at the speedometer. Eighty-five. God, they were all gonna be killed.

"Wow!" Barbara said, "this is so cool. Like warp speed." She opened the window and stuck her arm out into the night. "This is *so* cool!"

With the road stretching straight in front of them, John increased the speed to a hundred, but now he kept over-steering so the car seemed to quiver and shake, pitching from side to side, threatening to fly off the road at any second.

As they climbed a low rise John allowed the car to drift to the right, the tires running close to the shoulder of the road, and as they came over the hill the stripes on the bike rider's back burst out of the dark.

"John!" Betsy screamed.

He jerked the steering wheel and pulled the car back onto the road past the bike rider, but the sudden change of direction at that speed threw the car out of control. It flopped onto its side and rolled over and over, and then seemed to leap into the air as it rolled and twisted once more. It took out a telephone pole which hit the car crosswise at the upper edge of the roof, flattened the windshield, and peeled the roof halfway back. The restraining cable on the pole snapped through the open windshield like a whip as the car came to rest on its wheels.

"Jesus H. Christ!" Larry pumped his bike to the car and jumped off. He pulled a small flashlight from his pocket and shone it into the car. Anyone with a less strong stomach would have been sick on the spot. Both the driver and the passenger had been decapitated, and everything seemed bathed in blood. He heard a groan from the back and he shone the light there. She was alive, still in her seat belt, and he moved to the broken-out window. The smell of gas was very strong.

"Are you hurt?" It seemed like a dumb question.

"I don't know. What happened?"

"The car went over," he said. "Do you hurt anywhere?"

"No. I ... I don't think so."

"Can you get out?"

"I don't know."

The phone pole lay directly across the car but somehow the wires had pulled free without breaking. The back half of the roof had been pushed upward and it gave him room to wriggle far enough into the car to release her seat belt. "The only way out is through here. Try to move, but tell me if anything hurts."

Betsy began to move, slowly. "I think I twisted my knee."

He had to get her out, and they were running out of time. The gas was pouring out of the ruptured tank, and when it hit something hot there was gonna be one hell of a bang.

He squeezed her leg below the knee. "Does that hurt?"

"No. Just the knee."

He shone the light over her face and head, and then her body. She was splattered with blood but he did not think it was hers. "This may hurt, but you need to get out of the car. I can smell gas and I'm afraid of a fire."

It was all he had to say. Betsy turned in the seat and lunged toward the window as he caught hold of her and pulled her free.

"Wait! My shoes! I lost my new shoes!"

"There's no time!" He picked her up never thinking about how much she weighed, and carried her away from the car.

"What about the others? What about Barbara and John?"

Larry shook his head. "They're not in good shape."

"But you have to get them out."

"It doesn't matter now," he said.

"What are you saying ... oh my God ... they're dead ...."

"I'm sorry," he said. "Just stay where you are, okay?"

She nodded, the tears streaming down her face now.

He took off his jacket, pulled it around her, and zipped it closed. "I have to go for help." He looked over at the car. "You need to get farther away, just in case."

"You can't just let them burn up...."

He knelt down and placed his hands on her shoulders. "Look," he said, "there's nothing I can do. They're dead and you're alive and you need help." He stared into her eyes, barely visible in the dark. "Come on." He helped her up and guided her down the road to where it dropped off into a drainage ditch. He led her down the slope and ran back for his bike.

He stopped and climbed down the bank to check on her again. "Just lie here and ..." the explosion sounded like nothing more than a big poof, and then suddenly pieces of the car were flying in all directions. What saved them was distance and elevation. They were just far enough away to be out of range of the bigger pieces and the smaller stuff flew past above them.

"Oh, God, God, God," Betsy cried.

He wrapped his arms around her, holding her tightly. "You're okay," he said. He held her close and stroked her hair.

"What's your name?" he asked.

"Name?"

"What's your name?"

At first she didn't understand the question, and when she did, she couldn't remember, and then in a rush, as if it were all one word, she said, "BetsyCrenshaw."

"I'm Larry Perkins," he said. "You're gonna be okay, but I need to go for help. Here," he handed her the light and clicked it on. "Keep this going," he said," I'll be back as fast as I can."

"Don't leave me...."

He heard the panic in her voice, and he lowered his voice and spoke as slowly as possible. "It's okay, now. It's over and there's nothing anyone can do for your friends. It will only take me a few minutes. You must stay here. Don't move. If another car comes wave the light around. Can you do that?"

For the first time she saw him. Larry the Rat. Never had she seen a more handsome face. "Yes," she said, "I can do that, but please don't take too long."

He grinned and squeezed her shoulder gently. "I won't," he said. "I'll go like the wind."

He started peddling the second he hit the seat, standing up and driving the bike into the dark, his small lantern lighting the way ahead as he peddled harder and harder.

She watched him go, shivering, her teeth clattering together, and then she remembered her beautiful new shoes and she began to cry. They were such beautiful shoes.

Even when he reached full speed he did not sit down. People died from shock. He peddled harder. I just hope she doesn't do anything foolish, he thought. He spoke with his mind, turning his thought into a wish and a prayer ... "stay where you are, Betsy, just stay there till I get back ..."

When he saw the lights of the house he peddled faster, straining his legs until he thought the muscles would tear apart. He rode into the yard, slid the bike into a sideways stop, leaped off, ran to the house, and pounded on the door.

He was greeted with the business end of a shotgun.

"There's been a terrible accident!" he said. "At least two people are dead. Call for help!"

The astonished farmer lowered his gun, his face white as he turned, picked up the telephone, and dialed 911. When he looked up, Larry was gone.

He laid the bike on its side, down over the bank where it

wouldn't get run over, and sat down next to Betsy. She was shivering hard, and he tried to remember his first aid course. "You need to get up again," he said.

"I c ... c ... can't move."

"What?"

"I'm too c ... c... cold."

He picked her up, surprised at how much heavier she seemed now. Adrenaline. The wonder drug. He carried her to the top of the embankment, laid her down, and then raised her legs and supported them with his own. "Just lie still."

He did not know how long he had sat that way, but it seemed as if it took hours before the farmer arrived in his truck with his wife who was carrying several blankets. She said not a word until she had gotten the blankets wrapped tightly around Betsy. "Just lie quiet," she said, and Larry thought he had never heard a more soothing voice. "The ambulance will be here shortly." She stood as her husband came back shaking his head.

Now in the distance they could hear the sirens and Larry took a deep breath and let it out slowly. "Betsy?"

"Yes..."

"How you doing?"

"I'm okay."

"Does it hurt anywhere else?"

"I think I may have hit my head."

"It's important to lie very still. I want to be sure you haven't hurt something that you can't feel yet, okay?"

She nodded and he reached up and stroked her forehead, brushing the fine dark hair away from her eyes. He'd bet anything she was sober, and he was pretty sure she hadn't been using drugs. What the hell had gone wrong here?

As he stroked her forehead, Betsy began to relax. He was so gentle and he was so brave ... he'd saved her life.

He watched as the EMTs put a neck collar in place, strapped her to a backboard, and loaded her into the ambulance.

The next thing he knew there was a man in a suit standing next to him. "Do I understand that you saw it happen?"

"Yes, sir."

"What's your name, son?"

"Larry Perkins."

"The chemistry guy?"

"Yes, sir."

"We met not too long ago. I'm Chief Watson?"

Larry nodded. "The school bus."

"Yup."

"Sorry about that."

"No need." He paused. "Can you describe what you saw?"

Larry nodded, wondering if he would ever not see the car rolling over and over, and then the two kids.... "It was awful."

"I never saw a worse accident," Chief Watson said.

"They almost ran me down, and he swerved and the car and went over and over before it hit the phone pole. The cable snapped through where the windshield had been. He shook his head and fought to keep from crying.

"Did you know them?"

"No," he said.

"How about the survivor?"

He took a deep breath and swallowed to hold back the tears. "No. She told me her name. Betsy Crenshaw." He looked up suddenly. "Somebody has to tell her parents she's okay."

"We'll take care of that."

"I don't think she was drunk or stoned."

The cop nodded. "How did she get out of the car?"

"I pulled her out. I could smell the gas."

"And then you went for help."

"She was in shock."

"How did you escape the explosion?"

"I picked a spot where we would be below the road."

"How fast would you say the car was going?"

Larry shrugged. "Over ninety."

"You sure?"

"I was riding at almost forty."

"On your bike?"

"I race."

The chief shook his head. "You're a pretty cool customer." He shrugged. "Who were the other two kids?"

"We don't know yet."

He looked over at the wreck. The firemen had hosed it down, and now it just sat smoking in the emergency lights.

"How badly were they burned?"

"Pretty bad." The chief looked at him closely. "I think you ought to have one of the EMTs take a look at you."

"No. I'm okay," Larry said.

"You want a lift home?"

He shook his head. "I'll ride," he said. "It'll help."

The chief clapped him on the shoulder. "As terrible as this is, Larry, some good came out of it. You saved Betsy's life, and now you know something you didn't know before."

"What?"

"That car could've exploded at any second, but all you thought about was saving the girl. That's what heroes do."

Larry bent over and picked up his bike, looked back at the wreck again, and then looked up at Chief Watson. "That's a nice thing to say," he said. "I wish I could've saved them all."

"But you couldn't. Nobody could have saved them."

"I'd rather not be a hero and have them all alive."

"So would I, Larry," Chief Watson said, "so would I, because now I have to tell their parents."

Larry wondered whether he could do that. He didn't think so. But the thought of it made something else suddenly come clear. This accident would change the lives of a whole lot of people, none for the better, despite what the chief had said.

Chapter Twelve

Coping

At school, on Monday, nothing was normal, but it couldn't have been any other way. The junior class met at a special assembly first thing in the morning, and those who had been closest to John and Barbara met with crisis counselors. The rest of the kids went to their classes, where the teachers encouraged the kids to talk about what had happened, hoping it would help them to understand, and in some way come to terms with the fear that sudden death always brings. The girls cried. The boys, with only an occasional exception, sat in stony silence. It affected them, and they felt the sadness and the loss, but despite the urging of the teachers to wash away their grief in tears, they did not. In fact, most felt no real grief, simply because the loss was not theirs. But it had an effect in the way it added a layer to what they knew about danger. It even introduced a small flash of doubt as it brought back the warnings from their parents.

Slowly they began to resent the attempts of their teachers to tell them how they were supposed to act, but they said nothing, and they refused to be drawn into what they regarded as hysteria. There were simply times when you kept your mouth shut and waited for things to pass.

Though Larry had not known either Barbara or John, after the papers on Monday morning carried Chief Watson's account of what had happened, they were linked forever. Everyone seemed to be watching him, and in an instant the fame he coveted weighed him down as if he'd filled his pockets with lead. He wondered whether he would have felt differently if his notoriety had come about in some other way.

Some guys, mostly the guys in his class, went out of their way to come up and shake his hand, but even some of the seniors stopped to acknowledge what he had done. He didn't know how to act so he just nodded, thanked them, and let it go at that.

Only when he sat down at the lunch table with Damon and the rest of the guys did he feel at all comfortable, and he needed very badly to talk about something else.

"Damon," he said, "what made Bunker change his mind?"

"I think maybe he was tired of losing."

"Now *that* I understand," Larry said.

The rest of the guys laughed, looking around as if they were unsure whether laughter was allowed on a day like this.

Then it was quiet, and Larry let it slide for a minute or so. Finally, he looked up from his hamburger. "Kind of quiet."

"We wondered if they went to the party," Warren said.

"I don't even know if they'd been drinking," Larry said.

"What about Betsy?" Damon asked.

"No. Betsy was sober."

They looked up as Joe Santos sat down with his usual two lunch trays. "What's up?" he asked.

"Do you think they were at the party," Damon asked.

"The kids in the accident?"

"Yeah," Damon said.

"Yeah, they were there."

"How do you know?" Roger asked.

"Because I saw 'em. They were flying, but Betsy was sitting on the stairs way at the back. She wasn't even drinking."

"What were you doing there?" Damon asked.

"Checking it over, man." He shook his head and leaned closer, lowering his voice. "I gotta tell you, man, it's worse than the rumors. The drug dealers supply the free beer, and then they walk around selling drugs." He shook his head. "It's a really bad scene. I just got a cup of beer and carried it around, and talked to people I knew."

"And John and Barbara were toked," Damon said.

Joe picked up his fork and dug into a pile of mashed potatoes. "Yeah," he said. "I mean, maybe they always did drugs, for all I know, but they were doing a lot of drugs when I saw 'em. The prices were really low."

"To get them hooked," Roger said.

Joe shrugged. "I guess."

"What'd these guys look like?" Larry asked.

"Big and nasty. Guys in their twenties. City guys. They acted a lot like my cousins." He set his fork down and turned toward Warren. "You know what kind of guys I mean."

Warren nodded. "Yeah. Wise guys on their way up."

"What the heck is going on here?" Damon asked. "I mean how does something like this get going here?"

"The Rumble Brothers," Roger said. "At least that's the rumor I keep hearing."

Larry set his hamburger down. "And now two kids are dead who might be alive, and that really stinks."

"We gotta do something," Damon said.

"No way," Joe said. "Tell 'em Warren."

"This isn't just the Rumble Brothers, Damon. You mess with these guys, you get dead. This is their business. You mess it up, they kill you. You even think about messing it up, they kill you."

"You're serious," Damon said.

"I'm serious, man."

"What about the cops?" Larry asked.

"Either they get paid to look the other way, or the dealers stay ahead of 'em," Warren said. "Sometimes they just don't care. They've got bigger fish to fry."

"Or it's too dangerous," Joe said. "Some neighborhoods in the cities, you'd need an army to go into them."

"Okay, I get the picture," Damon said. "But it sure sucks. I mean, two kids are dead, and there's nothing anybody can do about it? I mean, there has to be some way to stop them."

"Nobody has yet," Warren said. "It's too big, Damon. There's too much money in it. I know guys that ride around in Porsches and Ferraris. They have yachts. And suppose you're a cop. Cops don't make much money, right? Some guy comes along and offers you twenty grand to keep busy writing traffic tickets. Do you take it? Of course you take it."

Larry stuffed the last bite of hamburger into his mouth. "I just thought that the cops busted those guys, and that was that."

"Even if they did, they'd be inside no more than a few hours before their lawyers got them freed," Warren said.

"Did you know that car was gonna blow?" Damon asked."

"Not for sure. But there was gas running all over the place and the engine was still hot."

"And you still went in after Betsy."

"It really was no big deal, Damon. I mean, what could I do? I couldn't leave her there. But the truth is, I never thought about it. All I thought about was getting her out of the car."

Warren grinned. "This table is getting overrun with stars and heroes."

"Some hero," Larry said. "I was so scared my knees were knocking."

"But that's the point, isn't it," Roger said. "To do something like that, even though you're scared ... that's pretty cool."

"Nothing is cool," Larry said. In those three words he dropped a very large mystery into the conversation. He finished his chips, eating slowly, making them wait. "Cool," he said, "is what somebody else thinks, not what you think. Look at me. The least-cool guy in the whole school. Look at you guys. All cool, right? So why am I not cool? First off, I look like a rat, second, I'm short, and third I get good grades. And if anybody knew about my bike racing, I'd be lucky if anyone said anything to me for the rest of the year." He sat back in his chair. "What you have here, gentlemen, is a twenty-four carat nerd. But that's okay, because that leaves me free to do whatever I like, without worrying about what other people think. You guys, on the other hand, have to worry. Are you wearing the right clothes? Are you having a bad hair day? Do you hang with the right kids? By being cool you conform to a set of unwritten rules, and you know who sets those rules? The girls set those rules. They do it because it gives them a way to control the guys."

It left them stunned, and it was several seconds before Roger said, "where do you come up with stuff like that?"

Larry shrugged. "I've been on the outside a long time."

Slowly they cleaned up and headed for the tray line. He did not, Damon thought, know what the others were thinking, but he knew he was gonna come up with a way to stop this. His original idea had been to tell the cops about the parties, but if Warren was right, and some of those guys were getting paid off, they'd just tell the dealers who had ratted on them. No. What he needed was a way to set them up without their ever knowing they'd been set up. The worst part was that he was out of his depth. He needed to talk to Dad or to Mr. Waters, or some adult he was certain he could trust, and that was the very thing he couldn't do.

◆　◆　◆

He didn't feel much like playing football, he thought, as he pushed through the door and started walking toward the field, hearing the sound of his cleats against the asphalt. Maybe he had too many things on his mind, or maybe it was just that what he had on his mind was pretty depressing. And the worst part of it was that, because he was a kid, there wasn't a whole lot he could do. Even if he could come up with some plan to put those guys out of business, how was he gonna make the plan work?

And then suddenly Jenny was walking next to him.

"Hi," she said.

He smiled. "Where did you come from?"

"The girl's locker room."

"Cheerleading practice?"

"Uh-huh."

Several beads of cold sweat rolled down his sides beneath his practice uniform. Nervous. He was very, very nervous here, a little dizzy, and his vision seemed a little bit blurry. How could he be nervous just talking to a girl, when he could run a football team in front of a couple of hundred people, and never have it bother him at all? He couldn't think of a thing to say. Nothing.

"I talked to Betsy," she said.

"How's she doing?"

"I think she's okay. All she could talk about was how brave Larry was, how he pulled her out of the car, and then carried her to a place where they would be safe when the car blew up."

Damon grinned and shook his head. "Nobody knew about that guy, you know? I mean, he is one cool customer and nobody knew until now."

"He's kind of short, Damon."

"And I'm kind of tall. It doesn't make any difference. Size has nothing to do with it." He turned quickly toward her. "And neither does the way you look. It's what's inside."

"He eats lunch with you guys, doesn't he?"

"Yeah."

"And now he's one of the cool guys, huh?"

"Nope. The last thing Larry wants is to be cool. He just wants to be who he is."

"Whoa, now that's different."

"Yeah, a whole school of people pretending they're something other than what they are, and along comes Larry, who teaches me stuff I would never have thought of. And I'll tell you something else too. He can ride a bike like the wind. I never saw anyone go so fast."

"Betsy says he's really strong for a little guy. He just picked her up and carried her away from the car like she weighed nothing at all."

Damon grinned. "He's a really surprising guy."

"He's your friend, isn't he?"

"He's my friend."

"And the other stuff doesn't worry you?"

"What stuff?"

"You know."

He lied. He lied because he had to lie. "If people don't like me because Larry Perkins is my friend, then that's fine with me." And then, as he heard the words he had said out loud for the first time, he wondered whether he *had* lied.

"Betsy sure likes him, but I guess I'd like a guy who saved my life too."

"You think she really likes him?"

"She does now."

"You think it will last?"

Jennifer shrugged and Damon smiled. He liked a girl who could shrug.

"Would you ...." he looked up suddenly as he heard the coach's whistle. "Whoops, late, gotta go. I'll talk to you, okay?"

"Call me," she said.

He smiled and then broke into a fast trot as he headed for the field, wondering just how much all of this was going to interfere with practice ... and whether if the whistle hadn't blown, he would have had the courage to ask her to the prom.

And then Larry's words came back to him. "The girls make the rules." And what had Jenny just said? "He's kind of short, Damon." But it was more complicated than that because she had also wanted to make sure that he counted Larry as a friend. Did that mean Larry's status among the girls also depended on his status among the guys? It seemed to, but how could ever know? In fact, how could you ever be certain of what anyone was *really* saying? He shook his head. Stick to football. The rules are clear. He grinned. Or are they?

Chapter Thirteen

Invasion of the Name Snatchers

"You really think this will work?" Larry climbed into the driver's seat of his mother's red Mustang.

"I don't know, but at least nobody will know who did it. And if it saves one kid it was worth doing." Damon pulled his shoulder belt in place.

Larry put his seat belt on. "Okay. That's okay."

"I get the feeling you don't think this is gonna work."

"I always act that way. Drives my parents nuts. You know how people talk about the glass being half empty or half full?" He started the car, turned on the lights, and headed out the long drive to the road.

"Ah, no."

"Really?"

"Yeah, really." Damon sounded irritated.

Larry grinned. "I keep forgetting you're just a freshman." He pulled out onto the empty road.

"Right. Not even dry behind the ears as my father says. I don't even know what that means! When is anyone ever wet behind the ears?"

"When you're born. I get the same stuff. Never changes."

"Probably not," Damon said, "at least if you judge it by my grandparents. They still think my parents are kids, but they ride around on a big old Harley Hog. And my mother's mother dresses like she was fourteen, short skirts and everything."

"Whoa. Weird, huh?"

"Yeah, pretty weird." He shifted in the seat. "What does that mean, that stuff about the glass?"

"What it means," Larry said, "is that if you're negative about things, you see the glass as half empty, but if you're positive, you see it as half full. I usually see it as half empty."

"Maybe it doesn't mean you're negative. Maybe it really means that you can see how stuff could go wrong."

"Do you always do that?

"What?

"Turn negatives into positives?"

"I don't know. I never thought about it. All I know is that negative football players don't go very far."

"Do you think I'm too negative?"

"Not after what you did on Saturday. I mean, if you're negative you hesitate. On the field you just react."

"You never think about what might go wrong?"

"There's no time. All I can do is react to what happens. If a guy misses a block, I have to avoid getting tackled, but I still have to look find a guy to throw to, or I have to get the ball back to the line of scrimmage, or at the least, not do something stupid, like throw an interception. Do you see what I'm saying? Plans don't always work."

"Like tonight. We have a plan, but it might not work."

"What do you think could go wrong?" Damon asked.

"They spot us."

"How?"

"We don't mix in enough. They'd expect a guy like me to

be on the sidelines, but you should be partying."

"I won't even know who I'm talking to. I've only been here about a month, and most of the kids I know are freshmen."

"Just look like you're having a good time, I'll take care of the rest." He stopped at the red light, turning toward Damon. "And stay out of trouble. Remember, these guys carry guns."

"I got a game tomorrow. We'll stay an hour and then I gotta get home and get some sleep."

And at first, it all seemed easy enough. Larry stayed in the shadows, and Damon danced. He may not have known who he was dancing with, but they knew who he was, and all he had to do was hold out his hand and he had a partner. But despite how easy it all seemed, he kept his wits about him, keeping track of the time and declining whatever was offered. The next song came on and as he looked around for Larry, somebody grabbed his arm. He turned quickly to face a guy just a shade shorter, but at least three years older.

"Hey," the guy said. "You wanna watch who you're dancing with, you know that?"

Damon looked down at the kid's hand on his arm and then into his coal black eyes, and smiled. "Sorry," he said.

"You ain't got no idea how sorry you're gonna be."

He saw two other guys drifting toward them.

"I don't think you want to start anything here," Damon said.

"You think I care about?"

The kid was drunk or stoned or both.

"What's going down, Rodney?" one of his buddies asked as he came up to them.

"This jerk was dancing with Carol."

"He shouldn't have done that," the third guy said.

"Punks like this need a lesson," Rodney said.

Still Damon backed down. "I said I was sorry. "

Rodney squeezed his arm a little harder. "That's even worse. Probably you danced with my friends' girl friends too. You think you can do anything 'cause you're a big jock."

Suddenly Damon's voice changed. It was deeper and softer. "Take your hand off my arm," he said.

"And what if I don't? What're you gonna do about it?"

"Look, I don't want any trouble, all right?"

"You should've thought about that before."

Damon moved so quickly he froze them in place as surely as if their feet had suddenly turned to lead. One second he was standing there, and the next he was standing with his arm around Rodney's neck, holding his right hand twisted up against his back. The people stepped away, making a space for the trouble that was coming, but staying close enough to see.

"I think," Damon said, "that we ought to stop this before someone notices."

But there was no stopping Rodney. His voice hissed up out of his throat. "Get him!" he said.

The other two started to circle.

"Stay where you are," Damon said, "or he pays." He jerked up on Rodney's arm and pulled in against his throat.

As if from nowhere, two bouncers appeared. They were both over six-four, with arms like tree trunks.

"Let him go," one of them said.

Damon let go and stepped away, holding his arms to the sides. "Hey, I'm not looking for trouble," he said.

The second guy looked at Rodney and then at his buddies. "I warned you guys last week. Guess you don't hear so good."

"He was dancing with my girl," Rodney said.

"Maybe your girl was dancing with him," the second bouncer said. "The rule is, no trouble. People are here to have a good time, man." He looked over at Damon, sizing him up, knowing that despite his age, this was not a guy you wanted to tangle with. He smiled. "Just keep it cool." He handed out four reefers. "On the house, man, okay?"

Finally Rodney began to relax. He looked at the reefer. "Hey, that's cool. Hey, I'm sorry, man."

They turned away and seemed to melt into the crowd. Damon dropped the reefer into his shirt pocket and slipped off to where Larry was waiting by the door.

"What the heck was that all about?" Larry asked.

"Stupidity," Damon said. "Let's get out of here."

"Can't be soon enough to suit me."

The bouncer stopped them at the door. "Once you leave, you can't come back," he said.

"Gotta play ball tomorrow," Damon said.

The bouncer nodded, opened the door, and they walked out into the cool of the night.

They didn't talk until they were in the car.

"How'd you make out?" Damon asked.

"I got a long list," Larry said. "A very long list."

"You sure you can remember?"

"No problem. Photographic memory." He looked up into the rearview mirror. "I think those guys are following us."

"Head for Olympia Pizza."

"What's there?"

"My offensive line. All they do is eat and lift weights."

Two blocks down, Larry turned, and then a half block later, he pulled into the parking lot of the Olympia. The car was right behind them now, and as they climbed out, the three guys came rushing up to them carrying baseball bats.

"You punks are gonna pay for that," Rodney said as he moved in closer. But he knew how strong Damon was, and he decided to target Larry. It was a bad idea. Larry, nimble as a dancer, avoided the bat and went airborne, sending his foot into Rodney's face with a tremendous crunch.

Rodney went down as if he'd been shot, his nose smashed flat against his face, blood pouring from both nostrils. "Holy shit!" Rodney screamed. "I'm bleeding! I'm bleeding!"

No one moved. And then suddenly the parking lot seemed

to fill up with giants as nearly half the football team poured out into the night, gathering in a half-circle around them.

The other two dropped their bats, eyes wide, waiting to find out how badly they were going to get hurt.

"Pick him up and get out of here," Damon said.

They stood Rodney up, helped him back to the car, jumped in, and sped away.

"Jeez, Damon," Melvin said. "What'd you hit him with?"

Damon grinned. "I didn't touch him." He put his hand on Larry's shoulder. "He ran into the karate kid here."

"You did that?" Joe Santos shook his head.

Larry smiled. "A little guy has to have an equalizer."

"What're you, a black belt or something?" Melvin asked.

"Third degree."

"Let me see if I'm getting this picture right here," Joe Santos said. "We got this guy who thinks he looks like a rat, and who everybody thinks is like a major nerd, but then we find out he's bike racer, a hero, and a third-degree black belt. So what was supposed to be true is still true, except that part of it isn't." He clapped Larry on the shoulder. "We got plenty of pizza left inside. You hungry?"

"Starved," Larry said.

The cops pulled into the parking lot before they could get inside, and Larry stepped close to Damon. "You still got that joint in your shirt pocket?"

"What?"

"The joint the guy gave you. Get rid of it! Fast!"

Damon slipped it out of his pocket, crumpled it apart, and let the marijuana fall to the ground.

The two cops had a bad case of the swaggers. "Which one of you is Foxrucker?" the bigger of the two asked.

"I am," Damon said.

"The rest of you get inside. This is just with Foxrucker."

They waited until they were alone.

"What's this all about?" Damon asked.

"Maybe you oughta tell us."

"Tell you what?" His knees were shaking.

"It'll be a lot easier on you if you confess."

"Confess to what?"

The cop stepped up close to him and stuck his night stick into Damon's stomach. "I'm pretty tired of dealing with wise-ass, you know that? Every Friday and Saturday night it's the same thing. But this time we got you."

Damon did not recognize either man, and he wondered how long they had lived in town. He took a deep breath and tried to stay calm. "Can you tell me what's going on?"

"You know what it's about," the shorter cop said.

"We got a tip," the big cop said. He pushed a little harder on the nightstick.

Damon stepped back and the cop closed on him again, pushing harder on his night stick. "We got a tip that you're using drugs." He reached up and stuck his fingers into Damon's shirt pocket, his eyes growing wide when he didn't find what he was looking for. "Okay, what'd you do with it!"

Now Damon understood. He'd been set up.

"I think you've got the wrong guy," Damon said.

"Yeah, well, maybe I'll let your lawyer sort that out."

Damon glanced at the guys standing inside, looking out the window, and the shorter cop followed his gaze. "Charlie," he said. "Maybe we better check into this a little more."

Charlie ignored his partner. "We got him dead to rights."

The stick was beginning to hurt. But what could he do? The guy was a cop! The shorter guy was acting very nervous, and suddenly Damon made the connection. He had maybe twenty-five witnesses. "Don't poke me again," Damon said.

"What? You, think you're tough? You don't even know what tough is, kid."

"Charlie, we gotta talk this over, right now!"

"Get outta here, Mike, there's nothing to talk about. We just take him in and they search him at the station."

The short cop didn't give up. He grabbed Charlie by the arm and pulled him away. "Look around!"

Charlie looked at the kids standing inside the Olympia.

"Get the picture?" Mike said.

"What picture?"

"Witnesses, Charlie. You been using your night stick and he's got maybe twenty witnesses."

The door opened and the kids came outside.

"I told you to stay inside!" Charlie shouted. But they ignored him, and suddenly the cops were surrounded by a lot of very large kids and one skinny, short guy.

"All of you, back inside!" Charlie shouted.

"This is a public place," Larry said.

"I'm a cop! You do what I say!"

Mike grabbed Charlie by the arm again, and he was a lot stronger than he looked. He nearly dragged his partner to the cruiser, pushed him inside, and shut the door. He walked quickly to the driver's side, climbed in and drove off.

"What the hell was that all about?" Larry asked.

"Somebody tried to set me up," Damon said. "He went right for my shirt pocket." He shook his head. "Man, it's a good thing you remembered."

"Who set you up?" Joe asked.

Damon shrugged. "I don't know, but I'd guess it was the Rumble Brothers." He clapped Larry on the shoulder. "Let's get something to eat and I'll tell you what happened."

As they followed the others inside, Larry looked up at him. "How do you stay so calm?"

"I'm not. I'm totally pissed."

Chapter Fourteen

A Bump in the Road

Game day. Watertown High at home. The word was that these guys had a great defense, but their offense sucked. Damon finished tying his shoes and walked to the front of the locker room where the rest of the team had gathered to wait for Coach Bunker's pregame talk. In his mind Damon ran through the pass plays, wishing he had something more deceptive. If the Watertown defense was as good as they'd heard, he was gonna need something tricky, something they couldn't see coming.

Coach opened the door to the locker room and walked to the front. "Okay, this is the way it stacks up. The word is out that we can win football games so from now on everybody will be laying for us. What they'll be looking to do is get into the backfield and get to Damon before he can throw. That means the defense is going to over-commit, the linebackers shooting the gaps in the line, the ends slashing toward the middle. That gives us a chance to run our wide options and to pull the guards and trap the linebacker coming through with a block from the second back. We've worked on that in practice and it'll work.

But only if each one of you does his job. This is the key to the game. This is how we make their linebackers and ends hesitate. This is how we give our receivers enough time to get down field. Now go out there and raise some hell!"

They jogged from the locker room, down the road to the field, and finally across the end zone and onto the field, ready to play, ready to win. The roar of the crowd almost froze them in place. Last week there had been no more than a hundred people. Now the stands were filled, and there were even people sitting on the low knoll that rose up behind the north end zone. The word was out. Wally's Falls was ready to kick a little ... well maybe even a lot of butt, and everybody wanted to watch.

It was like being stuck in a pressure cooker, and even the kids who had played the last three years kept turning their heads to look at the crowd. The only big crowds they'd seen had been at away games, and that was nothing like having to perform for what looked like half the town of Wally's Falls. The fact that the crowd was all on their side made little difference to a team that had only won a single game. The message couldn't have been clearer. The crowd was there to see them win, and despite having won the week before, as a team they still did not believe they could win. There is a very fine line in sports between confidence and cockiness, but there is a very thick line between uncertainty and confidence.

Damon's stomach felt empty as he listened to the noise. During the passing drills, throws that he usually completed without a thought now flew wide left or right, and several times the ball seemed to ride with its nose up, fighting the air, hanging where it could be easily picked off. He knew why. He had simply never before done anything in front of so many people. And there was no escape. They had come to see the team win, but that meant they had come to see him throw the football. Worse he had not seen this as a possibility. But how? How could he have not thought ahead far enough to suspect that this would occur?

He was so addled by it that he didn't remember the kickoff, or who had returned it. One second he had been warming up on the sidelines and the next he was on the field, standing over his center, reeling off the count, taking the snap, swiveling, handing the ball to Harry, carrying the fake, the crowd roaring as Harry broke free and went twelve yards. It was like a dream.

As quickly as they were up, they were down. The next two plays went nowhere, leaving them at third down with nine yards to go for a first down. Time to throw the ball. He called a post pattern for Warren, and as he came up to the center, he checked the defense. They were looking for it. He could see the eyes on the right linebacker shift toward Warren, but it was too late to change the play because he'd taken too much time in the huddle.

He took the snap and the linebacker slashed to the left, hitting Warren, and taking him out of the play. Damon dropped into the pocket, spotting Roger. But he had two guys on him and the defense was coming fast. He spun, sprinted to his right, slipped a tackler, and then tried to throw the ball out of bounds. But he got under the ball and the nose turned up, leaving it hanging in the air like some big ripe fruit, and the defensive back picked it off. There was nobody between him and the end zone. In a blink they were down seven to nothing.

He waited on the sideline, standing next to Coach Bunker, his helmet tucked under his arm. It was no big deal. Everybody threw an interception now and then. He shook his head. It *was* a big deal. It was a very big deal. He hadn't thrown a ball that badly since he was eleven. He watched Warren take the kickoff and start upfield, dodging tacklers until he simply ran out of room. The defense collared him at the forty.

"Damon," Bunker said, "keep it on the ground for now. Even if they stop the first two plays, stay on the ground. They'll be looking for the pass and we can suck them in."

"Okay, Coach." Damon pulled on his helmet and trotted onto the field, almost relieved that he wouldn't have to throw.

He wasn't sure he could hit a receiver if the guy was standing still. They picked up three yards on each play and then, when they expected him to pass, he faded back into the pocket, and when the defense had committed to rushing him, he handed the ball to Tags, and there was the hole, right where Coach had said it would be. Harry tore off fifteen yards before they stopped him. In the huddle Damon called the same play on a quick count, and the second the ref whistled for play to start they snapped the ball. This time he faded back an extra step before handing off to Tags. Harry was pumped and he ran right over the first tackler and went eighteen yards.

Again, Damon wasted little time in the huddle. He called two plays and the first time he went with a quick count, running the option right, faking the pitch, and then cutting back, stiff-arming the safety, and gaining ten yards. They didn't huddle, but went to their positions and took their set as he called the signals. But this time he staggered the count and the Watertown right guard jumped offsides. Five more yards.

Still he did not huddle, using the play he had called before. Fifty-two slant. Tags took it for five yards. They were on Watertown's twenty-seven, and he could smell the end zone from here. As they dropped into the huddle Watertown called a time out, and Damon trotted to the sidelines to talk to Coach Bunker.

"Way to go, Damon," Coach said, "way to go!"

He could hear the crowd behind him, but somehow it didn't seem as loud as it had before.

"You ready to throw?" Coach asked.

"Only when I have to," Damon said.

"What have you got in mind?"

"We've run all our options right so far. Maybe we ought to try the left side."

"What do you think their coach is telling them to look for?"

Damon grinned. "Option left, maybe a pass."

"So what's the solution?"

"Option right, tackle slant, screen pass on third if we don't pick up any yards."

"Or ...?"

"Option left instead of the pass. I could also fake the pitch and then drop two steps and hit the back when he clears the linebackers."

Coach Bunker smiled. "I like the way you think, Foxrucker, I really like the way you think. Now, go get 'em!"

As well as everything had worked before, suddenly nothing worked. Watertown had its linebackers close to the line now, and even the secondary had pulled way in.

They gained only six yards on two downs, and on third down they ran the screen pass, option left. On the run, moving left, with the defense holding until they saw which way he went, Damon suddenly pivoted, dropped a step, and lobbed the ball over the linebackers to Tags who somehow managed to turn the wrong way, looking over his left shoulder instead of his right. The ball simply went past him and dropped to the ground.

Coach sent in the field goal kicker, Bobby Barton, who had a leg like a T-Rex. It should have been a done deal, a no sweat chance to score, but the snap was just the least bit off line and the holder, Sam Jackson, didn't get the ball straight up. The kick went wide as the crowd groaned.

But the Wally's Falls defense was ready and they simply stuffed Watertown's offense and forced them to punt.

In the huddle Damon looked over at Harry. "Tags," he said, "we're running the fifty-three, but this time fake into the hole and then follow my block."

The snap came back fast and he pivoted left, handed the ball off with his left hand, and then whirled and broke through the line to cross body block the linebacker. It worked and Harry blew past him. Twenty yards later the secondary caught up with him, but Harry was so strong, it took them another ten yards to bring him down.

But once again the Watertown defense was as good as advertised. They adjusted, and two plays later it was time to pass. There simply was no other option. He called the play, sending three guys into the right zone, and then he took the snap, stepped back into the pocket, seeing Roger get a step on his man, and he uncorked the pass. It was a throw he always made. You picked a spot and threw to it, and the receiver would be there. But it didn't work. Roger was where he should've been, but the pass went over his head by four feet. All they could do was punt.

They seemed to sleepwalk their way through the rest of the half. The only thing that saved them was that Watertown's offense stunk up the field worse than Wally's Falls. And the crowd was getting restless. They'd come to see a massacre and instead they were falling asleep. They'd come to see the new whiz kid throw the football, and he'd treated them to an interception and not a single complete pass. Zip for ten.

He sat in the locker room, head down, half-listening to Bunker. The man was like an animated fireplug, stamping and hollering, waving his arms, but Damon hardly heard him. What was he doing wrong? Was it the way he was gripping the ball? Or was he bringing his arm back too far? Or maybe it was the way he stepped into the throw. It had to be that. When something went wrong like this the trouble was always in the feet. How many times had he heard his father say that? Probably he was overstriding when he threw. That had to be it. Whenever you took too long a step, the ball was late coming through and you tended to drop your arm out from under it. He could work on that when they went out to warm up for the second half.

But as they trotted out onto the field, he grew less certain. His father was waiting for him, standing behind the bench, his hands in his pockets, wearing a tee shirt that read "Your junk is my next creation." He smiled. "You figure it out yet?" he asked.

"I don't know, Dad, maybe it's in my feet."

Harley tapped his head with his index finger. "Think small," he said. "Narrow it down. This game is played with a ball. Think about the ball, just the ball, nothing else."

Damon nodded. "I think I've been overstriding," he said.

Harley nodded. "Damon, just think about the ball."

"I must be overstriding ...."

"Damon!'

He looked at his father.

"Did you hear what I said?"

"Uh, I think so, I...."

"Think about the ball, just the ball, nothing else."

He grinned. "Got it."

"Can you do it?"

"I'll try." Damon glanced nervously at the crowd.

Harley clapped him on the shoulder. "Damon, every time you play, you learn, but you only really learn when things don't go right. Every day you write your own history. Don't think about the first half, think about the next play. Use that to make the next layer of history. Think about the ball. Think about what it looks like in the air after it comes off your hand. Okay?"

"Okay, Dad."

"And if it doesn't work?"

"Keep throwing until it does." He shook his head. "Coach won't like that."

Harley shrugged. "A week ago that didn't bother you."

Damon shrugged.

In the stands his grandmother said to Grace, "now, they're both shrugging. Grace, dear, you really must get them to stop."

Grace shrugged.

"Go get 'em, Damon," Harley said.

Damon nodded, jogged over to the bench, and picked up a ball. He looked at it carefully, then wrapped his hand around it, feeling the texture of the leather and the way the ball seemed to fit his hand as he flexed the muscles against the hard surface. He stood by the sideline, holding the ball, making it part of his hand.

"Hey Rog," he called. "Warm me up."

Roger dropped back several yards and Damon fell into a rhythm as old as he could remember, his feet setting up his body, and then his arm coming through and the ball leaping into the air, spiraling perfectly into Roger's hands. He threw another and then another, each time thinking about what the ball should look like in the air. And now, every time he threw the ball it went true, on target, bullets spiraling through the warm September afternoon.

They kicked off to Watertown to start the second half and Damon watched the defense go to work, without seeing the game. Instead, he saw the ball, and his passes flying, and then suddenly he was up, and pulling on his helmet as he trotted onto the field.

Coach had given him the plays he wanted to run, but when he got to the huddle Damon bent over and called a post pattern to Warren.

Watertown never saw it coming. Even if they had seen it coming they probably could not have stopped it. Warren shot off the line, ready this time, and he dipped his shoulders as if he were going right, leaving the defensive back in the dust. He broke into the secondary and sprinted for the goal line, turning his head as the ball sailed in above his shoulder. He simply folded it in and ran, and in the open nobody could catch him.

A kickoff, three plays, and a punt, and they had the ball back, and now Damon was on track. He played as if he were in a vacuum. He saw only the ball and those players he needed to make the ball move down the field. One pass had opened up the game. Now the linebackers couldn't cheat on the running backs by coming up to fill the holes. They had to hold back and watch for the tight end coming across or pick up a receiver going out and curling back.

After the second touchdown, Coach took him aside. "Damon," he said, " I don't know how you know what to do, but you do. That first pass play was a good call. If we'd run, they'd have stuffed us. So for the rest of the game you call your own plays. You run the team on the field. I've never done this before, but I think you can handle it."

"Thanks, Coach," he said. "I'll do my best."

"I know that." Coach Bunker shook his head. "What I'd like to know is what your dad said to you at the half."

"He told me to think about the ball. Clear my head."

"Saying it is one thing."

Damon smiled. "This is my game. I'd rather play football than do anything. I think the crowd got to me."

"And now?"

He shrugged. "What crowd?"

"What do you need from me?" Coach Bunker asked.

"Next practice I need help on my handoffs. They don't feel crisp enough. And I need more passing plays."

"You want *me* to design passing plays for you?"

"Something that uses a controlled scramble."

"We may need to go to a pro set. Tough to learn."

"These guys can do it. The more looks we have the better. All Harry needs is a step at the line, and he's got five yards every time. My pass plays all look like pass plays. The other teams will catch on after a while."

"I'll work on it." He smiled and he wondered to himself if he had ever, in all the years of playing and coaching football, had so much fun. He didn't think so. "Now you get back out there and run your football team."

"Yes, sir," Damon said. He pulled on his helmet and trotted onto the field as the crowd roared a greeting.

He did not disappoint them or his coach or his team. It was a blowout. After that it was hard for anyone in the school to think of Damon Foxrucker as a freshman.

Chapter Fifteen

The Sting of Victory

Damon climbed onto the empty school bus with his father's words still hammering at him. As always he was the first kid on the bus, and that gave him a little time to gather himself, to get his anger under control.

And he was truly pissed. Who wouldn't be? All he'd done was say that he wanted a ride to school instead of taking the bus, and his father had delivered the longest lecture in his history of being a father. It was a new lecture, and full of accusations about things he'd never done. Totally unfair. Just because he didn't want to ride the school bus didn't mean he had a swelled head. And even if he did have a swelled head, so what! He'd earned it. He was the star of the team, for God's sake. And stars did not ride on school buses with little kids or geeks who couldn't get a ride. And they didn't have to take crap from anyone because that's what it meant when you were a star.

He sighed, shook his head, turned and looked out the window at the passing fields, and slowly his ears began to cool. Talk about dumb. Here he was all pissed off, not because Dad had taken him down a peg, but because he'd needed it. How dumb was it to think he was entitled to special treatment? Look at Larry. He was the smartest kid and the biggest hero in the whole school, and he didn't think people were supposed to treat him any differently. Dad was right. If that idea got into his head, pretty soon he'd be sitting on the bench feeling sorry for himself. The truth was he was still a freshman, and no upper classman was gonna take any crap from a freshman.

But was it wrong to want to taste the glory? What would it be like to have everyone look up to him? He wanted to roll in his success the way a horse rolls in the dust after escaping its stall in the barn. And wasn't he entitled to that? Look at what he'd done. To the victor belongs the spoils! Unless your old man is Harley Foxrucker. What was it he'd said? Yeah ... "when you're on top your enemies multiply like rabbits, and you have to work a whole lot harder to keep your friends." What the heck did that mean?

And there was more ... "If you let this go to your head, the next time you start overthrowing the ball, you won't be able to get your game back as fast, and then pretty soon you won't have a game at all." Why is it so hard to swallow that? Hell, even I know that's true. Hadn't he seen it when they were shooting skeet? One good round and you stopped concentrating and shot as if you couldn't miss, and then you missed every target.

The bus stopped and a bunch of middle school kids climbed on and sat in the middle seats. No one had an assigned seat, but the rule was clear. The older kids sat in the back.

Damon shifted in his seat by the window at the very back of the bus, wondering whether anyone would challenge him for having sat there when he should have sat several rows forward. He grinned and shook his head. He was doing it. Just like Dad had said he would. Dumb. Just dumb. He moved up to his regular seat, sliding in and leaning against the side of the bus.

Sure, he could have taken a back seat but why cause trouble over something like that? Wasn't it a whole lot smarter not to change? After all, he had nothing to lose here. The guys who usually sat back there had no other claim to fame. What kind of a jerk would take that away from them? Stupid question. And this way, because they would be expecting him to take one of those seats, they'd see him as a good guy. Or maybe they'd think he was some kind of wuss for not taking it. How did you answer questions like that? Again, he grinned. His father had answered it for him with his lecture at breakfast.

At the next stop a large group of high school kids climbed on, and for the first time he understood what had happened. No one ignored him as they usually did. Even the two senior guys who still rode the bus smiled and said hello. But the girls, even the older girls, seemed very different, treating him as if they were seeing him for the first time. Only last Friday they had looked right through him. No wonder Dad was worried. Stuff like this could go to your head real fast. He turned in his seat so he could talk to the guys behind him. "That party was pretty wild, huh?"

"It was cool, like really cool," Dan Fearing said. "Wow, like I can't believe the beer was free, man."

Will Jenkins laughed. "You should've stayed. It got really wild later." He rolled his eyes upward and shook his head.

"I heard you got into a fight with some guy," Dan said.

"It wasn't anything," Damon said.

"Those bouncers are like awesome, man," Will said. "Like professional wrestlers or something."

"I heard that the week before, they took some guy outside and beat him up," Dan said.

Damon shrugged. "There sure were a lot of kids there."

"Lots of kids from out of town too," Will said.

"Who do you think is behind it?" Damon asked.

"Gotta be the Rumble Brothers," Dan said.

The bus slowed and finally stopped and Damon turned and watched Larry walk down the aisle and sit next to him.

"What's up?" Damon asked.

"Me."

"What?"

"I'm up and I wish I wasn't. I stayed up 'til one putting together the stuff we worked on. Even my eyeballs feel dirty."

Damon wrote on his notebook: "Everybody's listening."

Larry lowered his voice. "The price of fame?"

Damon shrugged. Out of the corner of his eye he could see several older girls watching him, slyly, but still watching. Would everyone be watching him? Dumb question. Of course. Especially the teachers. They would expect him to set an example. That notion dissolved the fun that came from being famous.

"When you asked me about double dating for the prom, were you serious?"

"Sure," Damon said

"I'm thinking about it."

"All right!"

"I could still change my mind."

"Who you gonna ask?"

"I don't know yet."

"You want me to put out some feelers? See who might be interested? Girls love doing stuff like that."

"Okay." He wiped a hand across his forehead. "Whew! I don't know about this stuff. Physics is a whole lot easier."

"Are you really that nervous?"

"Yeah, is that okay? I mean, is it okay to worry about something like that?"

"Sure," Damon said. "Hey, it's always like this when you're thinking about who to ask. Sometimes you ask three or four different girls before you get a date."

"But *you* don't, do you?"

"Sure. That's just the way the game is played."

"Nasty game, man. Very depressing. Prozac express."

"You get used to it. Most of the time it isn't personal, you know. They've already got a date, or they're going out with someone and you didn't know about it. I never know who's going out with who. Stuff like that'll make you nuts."

"No wonder you're so cool on the field. I don't understand how you just take it in stride."

"I don't know. Maybe it's because I've got my monster truck to work on, I play three sports a year, and I don't much on the phone." He shook his head. "I hate that stuff. Who's in love with who, who's going out, who's a jerk, who's cool."

"I think I'm gonna owe you more than chemistry lessons."

"You don't owe anybody anything."

They rode quietly for a while and then Damon turned toward him. "That stuff you've been making, did you notice how the smoke hugs the ground? It doesn't seem to get much higher than about ten feet."

"So?"

"Make a great smoke bomb."

"Great, thanks."

"Geez, I'm sorry, Mr. Touchy."

Larry grinned. "No higher than ten feet?"

"Yeah."

"I never noticed that. Pretty curious. I wonder why."

"And you can barely see through the smoke."

"It is thick ...." He seemed to drift off, his eyes almost glassy and then suddenly he came back. "I went to see Betsy," he said. "She's coming to school today."

"Is she okay? I mean, well, her locker's next to mine, and I don't want to say anything dumb."

"I can't figure out how a nice girl like Betsy got into something like that."

"I don't know her all that well."

"I think she was just trying to be cool. It's the easiest way I know to find trouble."

"Maybe you're right about trying to be cool."

"I am right."

Damon looked around at him, watching him, thinking that if anyone else he knew sounded so sure of himself, he wouldn't have believed him. But when Larry said he was right, he was. Even so, he seemed pretty irritable. "Are you always like this when you don't get enough sleep?"

"No."

"Maybe you got PMS."

"What?"

"I said ...."

"I heard you." He took a deep breath, sat back into the seat, and slowly he began to smile. "That was pretty funny," he said.

"What was?"

"Your crack about PMS."

"I was just trying to get you to laugh."

"Well, it worked."

"That's good. It was gonna be a long ride otherwise."

As he walked into homeroom, Mrs. Clark handed him a note asking him to report to the principal's office. He turned and walked down the hall toward the front of the building, wondering what he could possibly have done to get called down to the office when he had been there only long enough to hang his coat in his locker. On the other hand, maybe Mr. Waters wanted to congratulate him for the way he had played on Saturday.

One look at the group of men gathered in the office dispelled any such illusion.

"Good morning, Damon" Mr. Waters said. "I think you know everyone here."

He looked around at the two other men, Coach Bunker and Mr. Watson, the chief of police. He nodded to the two men and sat down This did not look good.

"We understand," Mr. Waters said, "that you were at a certain party Friday night."

Damon nodded.

"We hear you had quite a bit to drink," Mr. Waters said.

"I didn't even have a glass of water."

"Not in a mood to party?" Chief Watson asked.

Damon said nothing.

"You know about the team rules," Coach Bunker said. He shifted uneasily in his chair.

"Yes, sir. I just didn't think that going to the party would hurt. Mostly I danced. I was there for an hour and then I left and went over to the Olympia for pizza."

"Where there was a fight," Chief Watson said.

"Three guys with baseball bats decided to beat up on us."

"Jesus," Coach squirmed in his chair. "Fighting, too?"

"No, sir. I wasn't fighting."

"One guy got a broken nose." Mr. Waters said.

"I didn't hit him," Damon said.

"Who did then?" Chief Waters asked.

Damon shrugged. "There were a lot of people there. It got pretty confusing." He looked right at Chief Watson. "Is there a law against fighting?"

"You can't go around assaulting people."

"Who complained?"

"The parents of the kid with the broken nose."

"And they said I did it?"

"That's what they said."

He should have been rattled, but he wasn't. He was pissed. "Suppose I file charges against that kid for attacking me with a baseball bat? Wouldn't that be pretty serious?" He had something else to bring up, but he decided to wait.

Chief Watson looked at the young man across from him. No wonder he'd been so cool on the bus that day. Moreover, he wasn't a kid you could push around. "What we're really interested in are those parties and who's behind them," he said.

"So was I," Damon said. "Because of the accident."

"Were those kids at the party?" Mr. Waters asked.

"I talked to some kids who saw them there. They said that John and Barbara were stoned, but Betsy was sitting off in a corner waiting to get a ride home."

"Tell us about the parties." Chief Watson said.

"They give away beer and sell drugs. In the hour I was there I was offered coke, crack, weed, heroin, and acid."

"Jesus," Coach Bunker said as he shook his head.

"That's why I went. I wanted to see if the rumors were true."

"And you don't know who they are?" Chief Watson asked.

"No. I never saw any of them before. The bouncers sell the drugs and they're all great big, nasty looking guys."

"How do they get the word out ?" Mr. Waters asked.

"They just start it like a rumor. The first time, everybody knew about it on Monday, but this time nobody knew until after school on Friday."

"Are you planning to go the next one?" Mr. Waters asked.

"No."

"You'd better not," Coach Bunker said. "If word gets around that you're partying, and I don't throw you off the team, there'll be absolute hell to pay. I can look the other way this time, but I can't do it twice." He ran his right hand back over his bald head. "Especially now, Damon. You may not like it, but you're going to find out that kids will follow you. Anything you get away with, they think they can get away with."

Mr. Waters grinned. "The price of fame," he said.

Damon nodded. "Dad went over that at breakfast."

"If you hear anything, will you tell us?" Mr. Waters asked.

Damon shook his head. "I can't do that," he said.

"Why not?" Chief Watson asked.

"These guys carry guns. If they found out who told, I could be in a lot of trouble. And the other thing is, most of the kids who were there would figure out who finked on them."

Mr. Waters rolled a yellow pencil between his fingers, his head cocked to one side. "We need to stop this," he said.

"Can you do it?" Damon asked.

"I'm bringing in the sheriff," Chief Watson said. "There won't be a building in town that won't be covered."

"That'll be better than Mike and Charlie," Damon said.

Chief Watson looked at him carefully. "Are we talking about the Mike and Charlie who work for me?"

Damon nodded.

"What have they got to do with this?"

"Somebody tried to set me up. They were giving out free joints and I stuck one in my shirt pocket and threw it away later. But someone tipped off Mike and Charlie and they tried to pinch me at the Olympia. Charlie reached right for my shirt pocket, and when he didn't find it, he got mean. He kept poking me in the stomach with his nightstick until Mike made him stop because there were about twenty-five guys watching from inside the Olympia." He pulled himself up in his chair. "What do you think my father's gonna say when I tell him that?"

"That sounds like a threat," Watson said.

When Damon looked across at him, Chief Watson could see Harley Foxrucker in his son, and he was surprised at how uneasy he felt facing a fourteen-year-old kid.

"I think maybe those parties happen because someone is looking the other way," Damon said. He looked right at Chief Watson. "Charlie knew right where to look, so somebody who knew me must have set me up."

Chief Watson nodded. "I'll look into it," he said.

"You better do a hell of a lot more than that," Coach Bunker said. "You got cops on the take, and they're out there pushing kids around. Suppose the guys in the diner had jumped your cops to protect Damon? Where would we be if that had happened? Would anyone have believed the kids? I gotta tell, you, Watson, if anything like that happens again, you got me *and*

Harley Foxrucker on your case!"

Mr. Waters held up his hand, "Calm down, Coach. We've all known each other a long time and none of us wants this kind of thing happening here."

"If I've got cops on the take," the chief said. "I'll find out, and when I do they're gonna be looking at sharing cells with guys they've arrested." He turned to Damon. "I'm sorry about that, Damon." He grinned. "But I do need to know whether I can expect a visit from your father."

"No, sir. I let it ride."

"Now why would you do that?" Mr. Waters asked.

"Because I think the bigger thing here is the parties." He shrugged. "I mean, two kids are dead and I don't want that to happen again." He sat back in his chair. "It's too bad we can't have parties where kids can drink a couple of beers, dance, and have a good time. They're good kids just trying to have some fun. It's too bad we can't have parties like that."

"But we can't, can we?" Chief Watson said. "After all, there are laws."

"Dumb laws." Damon shook his head. "Wouldn't it be better to control what happened and let everyone find out on their own? I don't mean with drugs. Just some beer."

"What you're saying, Damon, if I understand you," Mr. Waters said, "is that the kids aren't likely to be much help to us, is that right?"

"Yes, sir."

"Unless I'm mistaken, you've got something on your mind."

"Yes, sir."

"Would you mind sharing that with us?"

"I can't.

"Don't do anything foolish," Chief Watson said. "Because you're right. These guys wouldn't hesitate to kill anyone."

Damon nodded.

"I've scheduled a school-wide assembly for ten," Mr. Waters said. "I'm going to announce that anyone we catch at one of those parties will be suspended from school. I'm also sending a letter home warning the parents."

"I can ask the City Council for a curfew," Chief Watson said.

"It won't stop it," Damon said. "Most of the kids think the parties are the coolest thing that ever happened here."

"Tell me what will then, Damon," Chief Watson said.

"It'll stop when the kids don't want to go."

"And how do I do that?"

Damon shrugged. "I'm working on it," he said. It was clear from the look on their faces that they put absolutely no faith in a kid his age, or the idea that sometimes kids know how to fix things. In truth, he wasn't sure that his scheme would work, but he had to find out. Threatening them with suspension would help.

"Why won't you tell us where the party's going to be?" Mr. Waters asked.

"Because a whole lot of good kids will wind up in trouble over nothing more than drinking a couple of beers."

"And you don't think that's a problem, even though it's against the law?" Chief Watson asked. "How many of those kids can handle a few beers? How many will be driving drunk?"

Damon looked directly into Chief Watson's eyes, his gaze firm, his voice steady and clear when he spoke. "Some laws are dumb," he said. "The worst laws are the ones that keep kids from growing up."

"Perhaps you're right, Damon," Mr. Waters said. "But the laws are there to make sure kids *do* grow up."

Damon nodded. "Yes, sir, I understand that. I just think we need to find some way to do both things."

Mr. Waters looked at him carefully, realizing that he was only beginning to appreciate this kid. He was a whole lot smarter than his grades showed, and he was way ahead of them just now. Maybe he ought to go have a cup of coffee with Harley.

Chapter Sixteen

The Best Laid Plans ...

The Letter that Damon and Larry sent to the parents was simple. It said only that their child had been at a party where drugs were being sold and beer was free. It also said that the accident which had taken the lives of two kids occurred after those kids had left the party.

Even the Rumble Brothers got letters, and because business always came first, they skipped school and headed into the city to meet with Angelo in the back room of the Italian restaurant in the south end where he had his office.

Angelo sat quietly, looking down at the letter, his face betraying little, and then suddenly he balled the letter up and threw it across the room. "What the hell is this! Who did this?"

No answer.

"What's your guess? What's the damage here?"

"I don't know," Kyle said. "We came right here."

"Gimme a guess anyway."

"Not many kids are gonna show up," Keith said.

"Yeah," Angelo said. "That's the way I read it too." He shook his head. "I don't know what this world is coming to. You try to make sure kids have fun, and then some asshole ruins it." He leaned back in his chair. "Did kids in other towns get letters?"

"I don't know," Keith said.

He waved his hand. "Doesn't matter." He sat quietly for several seconds. "You know what this means? Lemme tell you what this means. This means I'm gonna have to take somebody out, which is very bad for business." He stood and walked across the office to look out the dingy window into an even dingier alley, and then he turned. "I need to know who did this."

Kyle shook his head. "The place was packed."

"Think about it. Who's most pissed off about the parties? "

"After the accident it could be anybody," Richie said.

He stabbed his arm at Richie, pointing with his index finger. "Now that's where you're wrong, see? It couldn't be anybody, because not just anybody is that smart." He picked up his cup of coffee, took a long swallow, and set it back down. "I don't stay in business by being dumb. I keep in touch. I watch. I think. That keeps me ahead of the cops. So I see something like this, I say, hey, Angelo, who's so smart he could figure out how to pull this off?" He set the cup down. "So you tell me. Who's so smart?"

"The smartest kid in the school is Larry Perkins," Keith said, "but the guy's a wimp."

Angelo put a finger on each temple. "The name rings a bell here. I seen that name somewhere? In the papers maybe? Would this be the kid who pulled the girl out of the wreck?"

"Yeah," Keith said, "but ...."

"And that's the same kid who broke a guy's nose in the parking lot of the Olympia."

"No, that was the football player. Foxrucker."

"You see the trouble here is, I pay you guys to watch. I'm paying you to tell me things I don't know, but I know more than you do. The guy you think is a wimp is a black belt in karate. And he is a guy who was not afraid to pull that girl out of the wreck, even though he could smell gas all over the place. Now we add smart, and this is our guy."

"He was at the party Friday, with Foxrucker," Kyle said.

"Yeah, and I read the sports pages too, so I know this Foxrucker guy is some kinda phenom football player who is very cool under pressure. So here I am sitting in the city, and I know more about what's going on in your town than you do. This is not good business. I'm not getting what I'm paying you for. It makes me unhappy, if you get my drift here."

"What do you want us to do?" Kyle asked.

"You're supposed to be the tough guys? So you tell those guys I know who they are, and you tell them to lay off or I'll put heat on 'em like they thought was only in the movies."

None of them would look at Angelo.

"So what's this? You scared of them two?"

"Not them," Kyle said, "it's the Foxruckers. There's a lot of Foxruckers around."

"So what?"

"His old man is a war hero. He was a Marine."

Angelo snorted out a laugh. "A Boy Scout. You think I can't handle Boy Scouts?"

"His grandfather sells motorcycles," Keith said.

"Yeah and my idiot brother-in-law sells Cadillacs. What's that got to do with anything?"

"All the big gangs go there to buy their bikes."

Angelo sat back in his chair, folding his arms across his chest. "Now, that's very good information. In fact it changes my plans. You still let them know I'm onto them, okay? But you leave it there. No threats. No rough stuff. You got that?"

They nodded.

"Good. I'm glad you got that, 'cause you seem to be having trouble getting stuff, and I wanna be sure you got that, 'cause I got a lot riding on this."

He looks nervous, Keith thought, and he wondered what

would happen if they had to fold this deal. And then he saw clearly what he hadn't seen before. These guys really did play for keeps. If you screwed up you didn't just get fired, you got erased. And if Angelo had to back out, he was probably not gonna leave a whole lot of witnesses behind.

◆ ◆ ◆

They rode most of the way back in silence, and then finally Keith spoke. "I think we're in this too deep," he said.

"Com'on," Kyle said. "What's there to worry about?"

"Once we talk to Perkins and Foxrucker, the cops come after us. Angelo can't count on us not talking, so we end up dead."

Richie laughed. "That only happens in the movies."

"Angelo can't leave any witnesses," Keith said,

"What choice have we got?" Richie asked.

"We don't do anything," Keith said. "That leaves Angelo thinking that Foxrucker and Perkins ignored him. Whatever happens next is up to him."

"It ain't right to back out of a deal," Kyle said.

"Don't be stupid," Keith said. "A deal means you both get something. All we're gonna get is dead."

"I really think you're scared," Kyle said. "I mean, like ready to wet your pants scared." He laughed.

"You're not getting the picture, Kyle. We're between Angelo, the cops, and the Foxruckers, and the only one I'm not scared of is the cops. And nobody's gonna forget that wreck." He swallowed the lump in his throat. "I gotta tell you, Kyle, John was a good guy. And because of the party he's dead, and the party was my fault."

"Hey, you didn't make him take the drugs?" Kyle said.

"It doesn't matter," Keith said. "I'm through with this."

"It ain't that easy, Keith," Richie said. "You remember what Angelo said right from the start. Nobody quits."

"I'm not going to jail to protect a scum bag like Angelo."

"Nobody's going to jail," Kyle said.

"And look at the money, man. Two grand a week! We just gotta get past this little rough spot," Richie said.

Keith sighed. "Just drop me at my house, okay?"

"I'll have to tell Angelo," Kyle said.

"You do what you have to," Keith said. "But you let him know that I don't rat on people, okay? And tell him I'm sending the money back. I couldn't spend it without thinking about John."

Neither of them said anything for a long time and then finally Richie spoke. "You're really gonna quit?"

"Yeah," Keith said. "I was thinking about it before John died, but that did it for me."

"It won't be the same," Richie said.

"Things change," Keith said, his voice quiet and sad.

"Are you sure about this?" Kyle asked

"Yeah, I'm sure."

"So what are you gonna do?" Richie said. "You still gonna hang out with us?" He stopped the car in front of Keith's house.

"Maybe later," Keith said. "Once this is over. Maybe then I then I won't feel so sad about John." He climbed out, closed the door, and walked away without looking back. For the first time in his life he felt good about himself. He was eighteen and it was time to make decisions. He'd made one and now he'd made another. He didn't even go into the house, but walked around back to where his car sat next to the garage. He climbed in, started the engine, backed around, and then stopped, looking out through the windshield at the back of the house where he had lived all his life. It was as if he had never seen it before. It looked different now, but he could not say how. It was just different.

It needed a coat of paint again, and he thought about how he and Dad had painted it the summer before he had started high school. It was only one story high, a ranch house, and not very big. It had been hard work but he'd liked it. Days when

Dad was at work he'd painted alone, taking care of the front and back where he only had to use the short ladder. On the weekends they worked together, Dad doing the gable ends while he painted the trim around the windows and then the shutters. He could not remember them doing anything together after that.

They didn't even go to football games anymore. It was as if everything that had anything to do with his family had been erased. Now he was eighteen and he didn't know how he'd gotten here. It was like trying to see through a frosted window.

He put the car into gear and rolled down the driveway, stopping at the street to check for traffic before pulling out. He drove slowly, distracted by what he had discovered, and then, as he drove, things began to come back to him. He remembered all the fights over hanging out with Richie and Kyle. He remembered all the trouble over his grades, and his parents pleading with him to work harder. He had ignored them. It wasn't important. He was passing, and that was all that mattered.

And once he'd gotten his license, he'd gone out almost every night. Cruising. Looking for trouble. He shook his head. How had they stayed out of jail? God, they'd done enough stuff to get arrested a hundred times over. Had they just been lucky?

The memories he had not been able to recall came flooding back. Fights with kids, fights with his parents, fights with his teachers. How could he have been so stupid?

In the center of town he parked in the municipal lot and walked the block to the barber shop where he'd had his hair cut since he was a little boy.

The barber, Mr. Sondstrom, looked up as he came in, smiled, and set aside his newspaper. "Well, now here's a customer I haven't seen in a long time."

"Hi, Mr. Sondstrom," Keith said. "I need a haircut."

Mr. Sondstrom looked at him, eyebrows raised as he studied his long, nearly shoulder-length hair. "Climb into the chair and we'll take of that," he said. He waited till Keith sat down, and then swirled the striped cloth over him, and wrapped a piece of tissue paper around his neck. "What kind of a haircut would we be talking about?" he asked.

Keith looked at him in the mirror, surprised to discover how much older Mr. Sondstrom seemed. His hair was white and with his sharp blue eyes and chubby cheeks he looked almost like Santa Claus. "Short," he said.

"How short?"

"Crew cut."

"Okay." He picked up his clippers. "How short?"

"Like the Marines."

"The guys from the recruiting office get their hair cut here. You want it like that?"

"Just like that."

"Are you sure you're ready for this?"

"I'm ready," Keith said.

Mr. Sondstrom turned on the clipper and started at the back, running a track right over the middle of Keith's head.

In the mirror, Keith watched a new person appear. With every pass of the clippers his face seemed to emerge from the dark. It was a face he had never seen before. He stared hard at the image, trying to find himself in the face he saw. He began to smile. He looked older. He looked ... like his father! What a surprise it would be when his parents got home. And when he went to school tomorrow nobody would know who he was.

Mr. Sondstrom finished by shaving away his sideburns and then the back of his neck. Finally, he swept away the cloth and smiled at Keith in the mirror. "Well, now what do you think! Short enough for you?"

"It's perfect," Keith said.

"You look like an All American," Mr. Sondstrom said.

Keith paid for the haircut, checked himself in the mirror once again, and smiled. "Thanks, Mr. Sondstrom."

"The pleasure was all mine," Mr. Sondstrom said.

Outside, he turned left, walked to the end of the block, and then halfway down the next block. He turned into the building without hesitating, stopping at the desk as a young man in uniform looked up at him.

"What can I do for you?" he asked.

"I want to be a Marine," Keith said.

"Sit down and we'll talk about it." He reached out. "I'm Corporal Sparks."

Keith shook hands and sat down. "Keith Jones."

"How old are you, Keith?"

"I just turned eighteen."

"Have you graduated from high school yet?"

"In the spring."

"How are your grades?"

"I'm passing."

"Okay. We have a whole battery of tests you'll have to take and a questionnaire to fill out, and depending on how you do, you can go for basic training right after you graduate."

"No sooner?"

He laughed. "Somebody chasing you?"

Keith laughed with him. "No. Nothing like that. I just wanted to get on with things. I don't like school much."

"Who does? But we think having your high school diploma in your pocket will make you a better Marine." He gathered a bunch of papers, took a manila envelope from a drawer of his desk, and slipped the papers into it. "You take these home and fill them out. As soon as you're finished bring them back to me and we can schedule the tests." He handed Keith the envelope. "What made you decide to join the Marines?"

The question took him by surprise. He hadn't thought about it. "I don't know. I guess 'cause whenever you hear about Marines, you hear how tough they are. My principal was a Marine. And Mr. Foxrucker too."

"You couldn't pick finer examples. Captain Waters was a

legend in Viet Nam and Sergeant Foxrucker won the silver star, the purple heart, and the Medal of Honor."

"I didn't know that," Keith said. "I didn't know anybody in our town had gotten the Medal of Honor."

Corporal Sparks smiled. "You're making the right choice, Keith. Even if you decide not to make it a career, you'll always be a Marine, and you'll share that with every other Marine." He stood up and Keith stood up as well, pulling himself straighter, squaring his shoulders the way Corporal Sparks did.

At the door he smiled and shook hands. "Thanks," he said. "I'll get these papers back to you right away."

"I'll be looking for them," Corporal Sparks said.

On the way home in the car, he felt that for the first time his life was going somewhere. But it still left him with a problem. Angelo. "Bang, you're dead." He shivered. How did you stop something like this? Or could you? Yes, he thought, you could. You got him before he got you. No other way. You just shot him. He shook his head, wondering if he could really do that. It was different in a war, but in a way this was a war. There was an enemy and that enemy was going to try to kill him. Wasn't that just like war, except on a smaller scale? He saw the difference, clearly enough. It was not a war. It was nothing like a war. Killing someone this way would be murder, and there was no way around that. But on the other hand, the guy was gonna murder him if he didn't stop it. What would you call it? Self defense? Would the cops call it that?

And even if they did, he was pretty sure the Marines wouldn't want him after that. Nobody would. Yeah. Somebody would. The guys Angelo worked for. They wouldn't let it go. So it would have to be murder. He'd have to kill him without anyone knowing who had done it.

He blinked once and then twice. What was he talking about? Was he out of his mind? Murder? He was thinking about murder? Thinking about murdering Angelo? How nuts was that?

Chapter Seventeen

The Message

Damon stood at his locker, trying to find his history book when he heard the locker next to him open. He pulled his head out and smiled at Betsy.

"How you doing?" he asked.

"I'm pretty good now," she said. "Thanks to your friend."

"He's the best guy in this whole school."

"You mean he's suddenly not the nerd everyone thought?"

"You got that right."

"He's also very brave."

Damon grinned. "Except when it comes to girls."

"He didn't seem shy to me," Betsy said.

"It's not that he's shy."

"You mean because he's not handsome."

"Yeah."

"And you are."

"Jeez, Betsy, did I say that? Look, Larry's my friend, okay? I also need some help here. He wants to go to the prom, but I think he's afraid to ask anyone. I thought you might know someone who'd like a date for the prom."

She looked up at him, studying him carefully, wondering why she saw him so differently now. She would have dated him if he had asked ... any girl would, but it wasn't the same. The funny thing was that now she actually liked him. "He did a lot more than just pull me out of that car. He's been to visit me every day, and that helped more than anyone will ever know. He is such a nice guy. He was really worried. Nobody but my parents ever worried about me like that." She closed the door to her locker. "The least I can do is get him a date for the prom."

Damon grinned. "He's truly a great guy." He looked up and there was Jennifer walking down the hall with two of her girlfriends. He took a deep breath, stepped away from his locker, and began walking alongside her.

"Hi," he said, "can I talk to you for a second?"

"Sure." She stopped.

He had to get this done fast before his courage failed him. "I thought, I mean, well what I wanted to ask you, is if you'd go to the prom with me?"

"Sure," she said. "I'd love to."

He smiled and then he smiled harder. "You will? Really? Wow, that's great. I'll call you, okay?"

"Tonight?"

"Around eight?"

"Okay."

He watched her walk away, standing in the middle of the hall until she turned the corner.

"What was that all about?" Betsy asked.

"I just got a date for the prom," he said.

"I'm surprised it took you so long," she said.

"What?"

"Everybody knew you'd ask her, Damon. It was just a matter of when you'd get around to it."

"How did everybody know that? I didn't even know that."

"God, boys are so dense sometimes." She laughed and closed her locker. "I'll get a date for Larry," she said.

"Yes! Hey, Betsy, thanks."

"No problem, football dude."

The mystery, he thought, as he dug back into his locker and finally found his history book, was how stuff like this seemed to work out. It was most astonishingly weird. He put his hand on the locker to close it, and suddenly there were two of the Rumble Brothers standing next to him.

"What do you guys want?" he asked.

"The man knows who sent the letters," Kyle said.

"What the hell does that mean?" Damon asked.

"You know what it means," Kyle said.

"I don't know what you guys are talking about. You wanna give me a little hint here?"

"He is very unhappy," Richie added. "He says if you don't stop, something real nasty might happen to you and Perkins."

Damon stared at them, angry now, his ears getting hot, which was a very bad sign, because when his ears got really hot he usually lost it. "What is this all about, huh? Is this about that crazy letter that everybody got?"

"All I'm doing is delivering a message," Richie said.

"Yeah," Kyle said.

"And you think I had something to do with that?"

"You and Perkins," Richie said.

He slapped his locker door closed and closed the lock. "You guys must be doing your own dope."

"Just be cool, Foxrucker," Kyle said. "Be cool and nothing happens. You like, dig what I'm saying here?"

"The only problem," Damon said, "is that you delivered the message to the wrong guy." He grinned.

They left him standing at his locker, trying to calm down, trying to control the anger and fury as he turned and headed for class, walking fast, because now he was gonna be late.

How had they found out? Could they have figured it out on their own? Was the guy they worked for that smart? We even dropped the letters in three different towns. Somebody must have been watching. But how would they know who to follow? Had they just figured it out? Suddenly everything had gotten a lot more dangerous and he needed to talk to Larry right away.

He was so preoccupied he walked right past his classroom, and not until the bell went off did he look up, groan, turn, and head back to the room.

Mr. Walker stopped his lecture long enough to mark him late, and then picked up where he had left off. Damon opened his notebook, took out a pen and tried to listen, but even when he had nothing else on his mind, Mr. Walker's lectures were boring. It was like listening to a window fan. The only good thing about his lectures was that it gave you time to think about other things. He looked up at the clock. Forty minutes to go. Forty minutes and then he had football practice and he could walk out to the field with Larry.

But instead, as he came out of the locker room there was Jennifer. She smiled and fell in alongside as he smiled back.

"How's Betsy?" she asked.

"She's okay. At least she says she is."

"I can't imagine what that must have been like."

"Me either." He shook his head. "Just really, really nasty."

"Who are we going to the prom with?"

"I don't know yet."

"We could get a limo."

"A limo?"

"And I need to know if you'll be wearing a tux."

"A tux? Are you supposed to?"

"No, but lots of guys do."

"Do you want me to?"

"I just thought it might be fun."

"Okay, then I'll wear a tux."

She grinned around at him. "Are you always so nice?"

He shrugged. "I guess I just play it by ear."

"That's cool."

"I can't believe I took so long to get around to asking you."

"I took a big risk, you know."

He looked puzzled.

"I turned down a senior and a junior."

"Whoa. How could you be sure I'd ask you?"

"If you'd waited any longer, I'd have asked *you*."

Now he looked at her very closely, not at all sure whether he liked that idea or not.

"Does that surprise you?" she asked.

"A little, I guess."

"Sometimes I'm a kinda pushy, or at least that's what my mother says, but I don't think it's pushiness so much as determination."

He nodded, waiting now, but not at all sure why.

"I also talk too much," she said.

"How much is too much?"

She laughed. "Well, we hardly know each other and here I am blabbing away." She walked with her hands clasped behind her back, studying the ground in front of her as if she were afraid to look up. What if she'd said too much, what if she'd scared him off before they even had a chance to know each other?

"It's okay," he said. "All I care about is that we're going to the prom and maybe we could go to the movies or something."

She smiled up at him. "I'd really like that," she said.

"We'll do that."

"I thought I'd scared you off."

He laughed. "What made you think that?"

"Because you stopped talking."

"I do that sometimes. Usually my big mouth gets me into trouble, especially in class."

"I heard about that."

"Really?"

"I also heard you went to one of the parties."

"Word travels fast, I guess."

"What was it like?"

"Scary. They got these bouncers who go around selling drugs. It's a bad scene."

"Did you get one of the letters?"

"Yeah." He clicked his tongue and shook his head. "Funny about that. I was there about an hour. I never even had a beer, but you'd think I was the king of the party-down dudes."

They stopped at the edge of the field. "Thanks for going to the prom with me," Damon said.

"Thanks for asking me ... finally."

He laughed. "I'll call you later, okay?"

"Sure."

He turned and trotted across the field to where the other players were beginning to loosen up. Larry was waiting for him by the bench.

"There's a party tonight," he said.

"Where?" Damon asked.

"Almost in your back yard."

"What?"

"About a mile past your house where the road bends left, there's all those fields. Right there."

"That's scary. You can see them from the road ... no wait! If you drive to the back of those fields, there's a big patch of woods, and there's another big field on the other side."

"How far is that from your house?"

"Maybe a half-mile."

"You could probably hear the music."

"And see the lights." He switched his helmet to his left hand.

"That land isn't in Wally's Falls, and there aren't any other houses for a good two miles." He looked around at Larry. "What've you got in mind?"

"I don't know yet."

"Maybe we oughta call the cops."

"No. We talked about that before, right? Too many innocent kids will get busted and the ones that run will be speeding. I think we ought to just wait and see if our letter did any good."

"It did one thing."

"What?" Larry asked.

"They know it was us. I don't know how they figured it out, but the Rumble Brothers warned me just before history ."

"You're kidding ...."

"I wish I were."

"But how? How could they have known we did it?"

Damon shrugged. "Maybe they just guessed? I was kind of obvious."

"This is like trying to catch a bouncing football."

"Huh?"

"You can never tell which way it's going to bounce."

Damon laughed. "You're learning fast," he said.

"Just not fast enough. I never saw this coming."

"Like my Dad says, 'you take what the game gives you'."

"Okay," Coach Bunker shouted. "Let's get to work here! We got a game tomorrow and we got a lot to go over! Everybody stretch and then give me two fast laps."

Damon set his helmet on the bench. "I'll talk to you after practice," he said.

Larry walked toward the bench. At least one thing was clear, he thought. It was time to be very, very careful.

Chapter Eighteen

Even Attitude Can Change

At ten o'clock, Angelo arrived in his black Porsche convertible. He pulled up to where Kyle and Richie stood, off to the side of the beer kegs, shut off the engine and got out. He nodded to them and then turned, his arms folded over his chest, looking out at the sparse crowd of maybe a hundred kids, none of them from Wally's Falls. He looked down at the grass, then turned to face Kyle and Richie.

"So where's your buddy?" he asked.

"I don't know," Richie said.

"Yeah, right. What do you take me for?"

"He quit us," Kyle said.

"He what?"

"He said he was through," Richie said.

"Through? You can't be through! You get into a deal like this, you're in it 'til I say it's over." He stepped forward and stabbed an index finger into Richie's chest. "You hear what I'm saying here? Nobody quits. You quit, you're dead, 'cause dead guys don't talk, understand?"

"Hey, Angelo, it don't matter," Kyle said. "He's not gonna tell anyone, okay?"

Angelo shook his head. "Are you really that dumb? Do you really not understand what I'm saying here? I'm saying that he is a dead man. The contract goes out on him tonight."

Dense as he was, Richie began to understand that Keith had been right. They were in way over their heads, and now he could feel his legs begin to shake.

"You two know what's good for you, you'll stay home where people can see you so you got an alibi." He turned toward his car, and then with his hands shoved deeply into his pockets he walked back and stood close to them. "This was a good deal here. We were making money. And now it's done and that pisses me off. I am not a guy who anybody should piss off. Nobody screws with me. Nobody gets in my way. Especially not some high school kids." He jerked his right hand from his pocket and both Kyle and Richie jumped back. "Now get outta here. Don't try to get in touch with me. Don't come around to the restaurant, because I won't be there. Don't do nothing till you hear from me."

They couldn't get away fast enough. They piled into Kyle's car and drove off, spinning the wheels in the grass and then leaving a long dusty trail as they headed out to the road.

"He's gonna kill Keith, Foxrucker and Perkins," Richie said.

"Yeah, so what," Kyle said. "They got it coming."

"Not Keith, man. I known Keith since kindergarten."

"So what're you gonna do, warn him?"

"I was thinking about it."

"Then he'll kill you too."

"I think we oughta warn Keith."

"You're nuts, you know that? You are truly nuts! You ain't gettin' the picture here, Richie, you know that?"

"Maybe the cops'll get to Angelo first."

"Wise up, retard, the cops ain't catching Angelo cause he's

got 'em paid off. How do you think he operates? He makes sure there's no chance of getting busted."

"Watson? You think he paid off Watson?"

"Naw. He's another one of those crazy Marines. You can't get to guys like that. He pays off the guys who patrol. And those are the guys who would turn up first."

Richie sat with his arms wrapped around his midsection, squeezing himself as if he were afraid he might fly apart, mumbling, "I gotta get outta here...I gotta get outta here...."

"Calm down, man. Get a hold on yourself."

"I'm scared, Kyle. I think he's gonna take us out too."

Kyle looked into the rearview mirror at the car that had suddenly appeared behind him. Was it following them? When he came to the next side road he turned into it without signaling. The car made the turn right behind them.

"Where you going?" Richie asked.

"We're being followed."

Richie looked back into the lights. "They're gonna kill us, Kyle! They're gonna kill us!"

"Punks!" He tromped down the accelerator. It might look like a nothing car, but it had a huge V-8 under the hood and he'd put in a racing suspension and shifter, and now they were gonna have to catch him, and the one thing he knew how to do was drive. He spotted the next road, drifted the car out just enough to flatten the arc of the turn, steered into it and dropped to fourth gear. As he came around the turn, he hammered the accelerator, and when the tach hit the red line he shifted to fifth, and floored it.

Richie looked back. "I don't see 'em! I think you lost 'em." Then he slapped his hand on the back of the seat. "No. They're still there."

"Hang on," Kyle said.

The road ran straight as a laser beam out into farm country, and Kyle held the pedal down, watching the speed climb to ninety and then a hundred, and finally to a hundred and twenty-five. All he had to do was hold it straight and try to think. Wasn't there an old stone quarry out here somewhere? He couldn't remember. "Richie, isn't that old quarry out this way?"

"Yeah." He looked back over his shoulder.

"Is it on this road?"

"No. The second crossroad. Turn right. The road takes a big dip and then it curves and comes out right on the edge of the quarry." He looked at Kyle. "You're gonna ditch 'em?"

"Yeah, just like a game of chicken."

The first crossroad flashed past. "How far?" Kyle asked.

"I...I'm not sure. A half mile...maybe. You'll know where it is because there's a white cross where a guy was killed by a semi." He looked back. "They're getting closer."

Kyle spotted the white cross alongside the road, let the car slow, then dropped from fifth to fourth gear, let the car slow again, and then drifted the car out and into the turn. In the mirror he saw the car track him perfectly, and he accelerated up to seventy and held it there. The road was narrow, and up ahead he could see where it turned to dirt. He slowed again, making sure he had the car under control as they ran out onto the dirt and the dust boiled up behind them. Up ahead, no more than a hundred yards, he could see the lip of the quarry. Now came the hairy part. The dust would hide them, but if you added in the dark, they would be all but invisible. He switched off the lights.

"Turn 'em on!" Richie shouted. "You'll go over the edge!"

He counted off the seconds and then hit the brakes and cut the wheel, putting the car into a long side skid, slowly turning and turning until it faced back the way they had come. The car behind them never changed direction. It went straight into the dust and did not come out of it until the car was airborne. They saw the lights pinwheel once and then twice, and then they heard it hit the bottom of the quarry. Seconds later it exploded, sending a great red flash into the dust.

They climbed out of the car and walked to the edge, looking down at the burning wreckage.

"Wow..." Richie said. "You did it, you totally did it."

"I think I'm gonna be sick," Kyle said and he turned away and began puking.

Richie waited until the retching stopped. "You okay, Kyle? Hey, man, are you okay?"

"I wet my pants," he said. "I wet my pants and I got sick." He shook his head. "I thought that only happened to wimps."

"Who cares? You saved our lives."

"Let's get out of here before somebody shows up."

They walked to the car and climbed in. Kyle started the car and drove off slowly. For the first time in his life he wondered if maybe he'd been on the wrong track. After all, you couldn't be that lucky twice in one lifetime. Maybe Keith was right. Maybe it was time to stop. No. It *was* time to stop. The next time he wouldn't make it.

"I think I'm gonna join the Army," he said.

"What?"

"You heard me. I gotta do something different before I get myself killed."

Chapter Nineteen

"And What Rough Beast ..."

Damon sat in Larry's lab, watching him heating and pouring various liquids. "What do you think they'll do?"

With a pair of tongs Larry picked a large flask from the heat and checked the thermometer. "Kill us." He removed the thermometer and poured the liquid into the rose-colored liquid in a large straight-sided beaker.

"Hey, I'm glad you're taking this seriously, you know?"

"I mean that's what they'd do if this was a movie. In real life? Nothing. They'll just go someplace else. They've got a good deal going, and it'll cost them nothing to set it up someplace else, so why worry about revenge?"

"Yeah but I don't think that's what will happen. I think this *is* like the movies. All they have to do is shoot one of us, plant some drugs and money, and that's that."

"What do you mean, that's that?"

"The cops will call it a bad drug deal, and the next thing you know the parties start again."

"Where do you get this stuff?"

"Why? Is it too crazy?"

"No. Just the opposite."

A phone rang and Larry pulled it from the pocket of his big white lab coat. "Hello?" He listened for several seconds before switching off the phone and looking up at Damon. "I think a new movie just opened."

"What?"

"Some guy just told me that somebody named Angelo Stompenado is going to kill us!"

"Did you recognize the voice?"

"No. It was pretty muffled." Larry peered into the beaker, watching the liquids slowly combine. "I'm gonna guess that this Angelo guy is the one who really runs things."

"I think I'm kinda scared," Damon said.

Larry shrugged.

"Jeez, Larry! Some hood wants to kills us and all you can do is shrug?"

Larry shrugged. "What do you want me to do?"

"Well, something ... anything!" Damon began pacing.

"I don't know what to do." He did not look up.

"How can you be so calm?"

"Inside I'm a seething cauldron of anguish and panic."

"How do you hide that?"

"It gets in the way of thinking."

"Okay, what are you thinking?"

"I think we attack. They won't expect that." He looked back down at the pale pink liquid roiling around inside the beaker.

"Let me see if I got this right. You think we should attack a bunch of guys carrying guns! I think you are flipping out here."

"Well the cops won't believe us. Our parents would think we'd totally gone south, so either we wait or we can go after them. If we wait then they have the advantage of surprise."

Damon began pacing more rapidly. "Okay, let's say we go after them. Let's start with where. Where do we find them?"

Larry looked at his watch. "At the party. It'll go for at least another four or five hours, right?"

"Just walk right in?"

"No. I told you. It's outside in a field, remember." He fished a piece of folded paper from his shirt pocket, unfolded it, and flattened it against the bench. "Right here," he said.

Damon looked down at the map. "Are you sure this is right? That's the farm that backs up to ours." He traced a line with his index finger. "Right through here there's a road."

"So we could sneak up on 'em."

"With what?'

"I don't know. I never thought about this before."

"You saw the size of those bouncers. And they're all carrying guns. What chance have we got against that?"

"Do you think this Stompenado guy is even at the parties?"

Damon threw his hands into the air and let them flop to his sides. "How would I know?"

"Okay, let's look at the facts. First, they carry guns. Second, some guy named Angelo Stompenado is out to kill us. Now based on that, what can we do? I'm not up to killing anybody, and I've never shot a gun."

"I'm okay on the gun part, but I don't think I could just kill somebody," Damon said.

"So we're back to where we started."

"Even if we were armed, we wouldn't stand much chance. We'd need to lay down an artillery barrage before we went in."

"Whoa, now that would be neat!" He shook his head. "I don't suppose you have access to artillery?"

Damon grinned. "Not artillery, exactly."

"What?"

Damon grinned again. "Let's take a drive out to my place. I want to show you something."

"Okay, but let me finish this up first."

"What is that stuff anyway?"

"I think there may be a big market for a special kind of smoke bomb." He grinned. "You gave me the idea." He opened a closet and pointed to a tray of twelve-ounce glass soda bottles, filled with a rose-colored liquid. "The trick was to stabilize the stuff and get it in the bottles before any oxygen hit it. Oxygen is the catalyst. I had to use a vacuum chamber."

"Do they work?"

"Of course. You just toss them and when the bottle breaks you get smoke; nontoxic, close to the ground, and impossible to see through." He stuffed his hands into his pockets. "I figure the cops could use it to immobilize rioters."

"And also people at a party."

"This stuff is pretty weird," Larry said. "It takes a pretty strong wind to blow it off. It almost seems to connect to the ground. Think we can use 'em?"

"Yeah, I think so," Damon said.

Damon opened the barn door and turned on the lights.

"What the hell is that? It's huge!" Larry looked up at the truck cab sitting nearly ten feet from the ground. "You built this?"

"With my dad. He builds 'em for guys who compete. This is a kind of demonstrator."

"And you can drive it any time you want?"

"Sure. But only here on the farm."

Larry grinned. "Suddenly I'm getting the picture," he said.

Damon pointed to the door of the truck. "You see that tube? There's another like it on the driver's side. They're pneumatic mortars. We use them to throw smoke bombs. Your bottles are a little small but we can make up for that by patching them."

"Patching?"

"The same thing you do with a ball in a black powder rifle. It seals the chamber so the gasses can't escape until the projectile gets out of the barrel. We'll use grease rags for patches." He opened a barrel and pulled out a handful of brown rags.

"How far will it throw them?"

"A hundred yards or so."

"Awesome!"

Damon grinned. "It's a lot of fun to drive."

"I don't suppose it's bullet proof."

"It's got one-inch thick-steel skid plates. From the bottom it'll stop almost anything."

"I feel like James Bond talking to Q about the latest assault car. And look at the size of those tires! What the heck does it weigh?"

"We've never put it on a scale, but Dad says probably close to ten thousand pounds. There's a lot of iron."

"I gotta say, your parents didn't seem surprised at all, that you were gonna drive it."

"Naw. I take it out a lot."

"And hey, I gotta tell you, man, nobody's got a grandmother who looks like that."

"Yeah," he grinned. "Pretty weird, huh?"

"And that's your grandfather's Harley out front?"

"He sells more Harleys than anybody in the country. I think he knows every biker dude who ever rode."

"Man, you oughta see my grandparents. They all look like they live in a church."

Damon set a ladder against the side of the truck and began climbing. "Come on."

Larry followed him up, climbing into the passenger's seat as Damon secured the ladder in the bed of the truck and slipped through the open back window into the driver's seat.

"Wait'll you see this," Damon said. "This is why it's most fun at night." He turned the key and the engine roared to life. It made an enormous sound and the whole truck throbbed with the power of it. Once it had warmed he flipped a switch and a whole array of lights began turning this way and that, throwing powerful beams of light in all directions. "It's for show," he said, "but it makes it fun to drive at night."

"So much for sneaking up on them."

He flipped off the lights and switched on a set of lights that only lit their way. "Once we get to the woods road, I'll turn those off and use the shielded lights. It's downhill most of the way so I can just idle along. There's a second field and then a second patch of woods, and when we clear those woods, we'll stop and launch a couple of smoke bombs, check the range, and then launch the rest. Then I'll turn on the lights and put the fuel to it. Big engine. Cat diesel. Thousand horse. Four-wheel drive, four-wheel steering, independent suspension, center articulated ... not much can stop it."

"How fast is it?"

"I think we could hit maybe eighty over open ground." He reached up and pulled a set of ear phones from a hook on the ceiling and handed them to Larry. "Better put these on," he said. "At high speed it gets pretty loud. You plug the wire into that terminal on the dash and then adjust the microphone. That way we can hear each other and talk without shouting." He took the second set of ear phones and snugged them over his ears. "And be sure you're strapped in or you'll get bounced off the roof."

"Wait," Larry said. "How do I launch the smoke bombs."

"How many did you bring?"

"Twenty."

"Good, we'll try one to make sure they work."

He drove out around the barn, aimed the truck toward the distant woods, and stopped. "Here's how you do it. First you adjust the range with that dial next to the glove compartment. Set it on a hundred yards."

Larry set the dial and the tube on the outside rotated into position.

Damon picked up a bottle, wrapped a cloth around the

bottom and then dropped it into the tube on his side. "First you patch it, drop it into the tube, and push the red button on your side of the dash." Damon pushed the button on his side and there was a great wooshing sound. The he turned on a set of extremely high power lights. They watched the bottle arc down range, dropping to the ground and immediately a black cloud of smoke spread outward.

"Yes!" Larry said. "They work!"

"Okay. Let's do it!"

Damon switched off the lights and they rolled slowly forward, following a well-worn dirt road that angled across the broad field. As they approached the woods, Damon switched off one set of lights and switched on another which only lit the road a few feet in front of them. As they entered the woods he switched off all the lights. The road, mostly sandy, was lighter than the woods on either side.

"Have you got a plan?" Larry asked.

"Attack!"

"That's all? I thought football dudes always had a plan."

"Armageddon! The end of the world!" They came out into another broad field and Damon stayed close to the tree line. "We need to get through the next patch of woods without them seeing us."

"Doesn't your father have any guns?"

"Sure, a ton of 'em."

"Maybe we oughta go back and get some."

"No way. He's real strict about guns. And besides they're all in a safe right there in the living room."

"I think I'd like to be able to shoot back when people start shooting at us."

"We're pretty safe in here. The windows are a special glass so they can withstand a rollover. I think maybe they're even bulletproof."

"Wouldn't it be better to know?"

"I'm sure they'll stop a pistol, but I'm not sure about a rifle."

Now, up ahead, through the next line of woods, they could see lights in the field, and they could hear the music even over the rumble of the big engine. As they came closer they could see people milling around and a lot of cars parked in total disorder. Damon stopped in the woods and drew his seat belt as tight as it would go. "You ready?"

"I'd still like to have a plan of some kind."

"Like what?"

"What is this going to accomplish?"

Damon shrugged. "Scare 'em off."

"But what good does that do?"

"The way I figure it, they'll never know what happened. They won't see us because of the smoke, and...."

"And ... what?"

"We crush 'em!"

"And what about this Angelo guy? The one who wants to kill us. Remember him?"

"Squash him like a bug."

"Yeah, right. We don't even know what he looks like. We don't even know if he's here!"

"He's here."

"How do you know that?"

"I just know it."

"But why? Why would he be here?"

"Because after the letter, things are probably a little out of control."

"Okay. Good answer."

Damon grinned. "You ready then?"

Larry tightened his seat belt. "Ready as I'll ever be."

Damon let the machine crawl down through the woods and then stopped at the field. There wasn't any wind to speak of. "Ready?" He picked up a bomb and dropped it into the tube as Larry did the same. "Fire on three. One ... two ... three!"

With a loud woosh of air the bombs shot off into the night sky . Seconds later they hit and the dense smoke spread quickly.

"Okay," Damon said. "Fire at will!"

They continued firing until all the bombs were gone, and then Damon adjusted the angle of his mortar and fired two more bombs, big flares that burst high above the smoke and lit the whole field.

"I love it!" Larry shouted.

Damon pushed down on the accelerator, and with an enormous roar, they burst from the woods and started across the field, aimed right at the crowd. He shifted to third, and the big Cat diesel began to howl as they picked up speed. Now they were bouncing hard over the rough ground, and it was, by any measure, exciting. In fact, Larry thought, he had never done anything even a tenth so exciting. He felt as if he were leading a Roman legion in a surprise attack, bearing down on the enemy in the biggest chariot ever seen.

Angelo couldn't see a thing. Suddenly he was caught in absolutely black smoke. And somewhere he could hear an enormous machine, roaring and whining, and it was getting closer and closer. He turned and took one step and then another, moving away from the noise, his heart beating like a hammer. Where the hell was his car? He'd been standing near it, and now he couldn't find it. All around him he could hear people screaming and howling and ... the music was still playing and he headed for that, bumping into people, falling and getting up, sweating hard in the cool night air as the roar of the engine came closer still.

From the cab, above the smoke, they saw people break free of the smoke and run for their cars. And then above the treetops they saw something else. Flashing blue lights coming from both directions on the road ... a lot of flashing blue lights.

"It's the cops," Larry said. "Damn there must be twenty cruisers!"

Damon turned to the north, and when he reached the stone wall , he turned back.

"What are you doing?" Larry asked

"Herding them."

Larry laughed. "Right into the cops."

I gotta get out of here, Angelo thought. There's cops here, I can smell 'em. He started to run and three steps later he ran flat into the side of a car and fell to the ground. He cursed as he reached out his hand and felt the side of the car. Slowly he felt for the door handle, opened it and climbed in. It was his car! Talk about luck! He started the engine and switched on the lights. They made it worse, the light bouncing off the particles in the air and nearly blinding him, but he kept them on. Inside the Porsche it was very quiet At least there's no smoke in here, he thought. And now I'm history! He put the Porsche in gear and started forward. He knew he had to reverse direction to get to the road, and he cut the wheel hard to the right.

But in the smoke he could not tell how far he had turned, and he managed to turn a full circle before he straightened the wheel and stomped on the accelerator. The Porsche leaped forward, broke out of the smoke, and the last thing Angelo saw was the biggest tire in the world as it crushed the convertible top of the Porsche down onto his head and snuffed him out.

"Damn!" Larry shouted as the monster truck rose up on his side and then settled back down. "What the hell was that?"

"We just ran over a car," Damon said. "It came out of the smoke and I couldn't turn in time to avoid it." He whipped the wheel around, backed up, and turned on the lights.

The top of the Porsche had been pushed down below the level of the windows and the tires had buckled to the sides.

"Do you think anyone was in it?" Larry asked.

"I sure hope not," Damon said. "Cause I'm gonna be in a whole lot of trouble."

"Maybe we oughta get out of here."

"We can't. There's too many cops and they don't know whether we're the bad guys."

"So we wait."

Damon shrugged. "Hey, we're the good guys, right?"

"I think so," Larry said. "At least we are as long as there was nobody in that car."

The smoke had begun to fade, and they watched as the cops herded people together. And still more cops kept coming.

"Hey, Foxrucker!" Somebody called from the ground and Damon opened the door and looked out. It was Chief Watson.

"Yes, sir," Damon answered.

"You know anything about this crushed car out here?"

The tone in Watson's voice told him how to answer. "Not a thing, sir. It was just sitting here when the smoke cleared."

"I recognize this smoke," Watson said. "This is the chemistry guy's smoke. Is he up there with you?"

"Yes, sir, right here," Larry called.

"Nice work. Best smoke I ever saw."

"You want us to come down?" Damon asked.

"You might want to know that there was a guy in the car. A guy named Angelo."

"How did you know about this?" Damon asked.

"We got a tip that Angelo was gonna kill a couple of guys because of a certain letter. But he tried to escape the police, and his car went off the road, and he died in the crash."

"Yes, sir," Damon said. "The worst I've ever seen."

"Why don't you head home. I'll talk to you tomorrow. After the game."

"Yes, sir." Damon closed the door, backed the truck around, and headed for home.

"Do you think Keith tipped them off?" Larry asked.

"Who else?"

"Why would he risk it?"

"He had to get Angelo. Those guys don't let you quit."

"So Angelo would have killed him."

"Yeah."

"Son of a bitch got what was coming to him. He killed John and Barbara."

Damon changed the subject. "Have you talked to Betsy?"

"Yeah." Larry grinned. "She did what you asked. She got me a date for the prom."

"Hey, all right! Who?"

"She asked me to go with her."

"Whoa, now that is rare."

"Took me by surprise I can tell you. Can you imagine? A girl as pretty as Betsy asking me to the prom?"

"It's like my dad always says, life is a bouncing football. Just when you're sure you can't miss, it bounces the other way, and then, for no reason at all, it bounces back right into your hands. Your job is to make the most out of every bounce."

"Does it work?"

"I don't do too well with the bad bounces."

"Do you think you ever will?"

"No."

"What then?"

"I guess you live with them."

"Pretty hard to do."

"All the good stuff is hard to do," Damon said.

"How come a guy who is just a freshman keeps teaching me things?"

"How come an old guy like you keeps learning?"

"That's an easy one. I learn because it's the only thing I'm here to do."

About the Author

Robert Holland has a B.A. in history from the University of Connecticut and an M.A. in English from Trinity College. He studied writing under Rex Warner at UConn and under Stephen Minot at Trinity.

He has worked as a journalist, a professor, a stock broker, an editor, and from time to time anything he could make a buck at. He hunts, he is a fly fisherman, a wood-carver, a cabinet maker, and he plays both classical and folk guitar.

While he was never a great athlete, he played with enthusiasm and, to some extent, overcame his lack of natural ability by teaching himself how to play and then practicing.

Sometime during college he decided he wanted to be a writer and has worked at it ever since, diverting the energy he once poured into sports to becoming not only a writer, but a writer who understands the importance of craft. Like all writers he reads constantly, in part because, as Ernest Hemingway once said, "you have to know who to beat," but also because it is the only way to gather the information which every writer must have in his head, and because it is a way to learn how other writers have developed the narrative techniques which make stories readable, entertaining, and meaningful. It also avoids heavy lifting.

He lives in Woodstock, Connecticut, with his wife, Leslie, his daughter, Morgan, his son, Gardiner, varying numbers of Labrador retrievers, three cats, two guinea pigs, and six chickens. Unlike Mr. Hemingway, he does not like cats.